GREAT BALLS OF FURY

FEDERAL BUREAU OF MAGIC COZY MYSTERY, BOOK 1

ANNABEL CHASE

RED PALM PRESS LLC

CHAPTER ONE

I AM the villain of my story.

I didn't mean to be. In fact, I've been trying my whole life to stay on the straight and narrow, which is why I moved far away from my hometown and became a federal agent in the first place. I thought the FBI was the perfect career for me. No magic or supernaturals. Just good, old-fashioned federal law enforcement, where I was on the right side of the law. Where I was undeniably *good*.

Then Thursday happened.

I was tailing a suspect through the streets of San Francisco—a drug trafficking case that I'd been working on for weeks along with my partner, Fergus. The suspect turned and fled down a dark alley, so I followed, ignoring the stench of rotting food that filled my nostrils. I was so thrilled to finally be on the verge of a break in the case that I failed to sense the suspect's true nature until it was too late.

Big mistake. Huge.

The suspect tackled me in the alley and, somehow—maybe it was my natural defense mechanism kicking in—he triggered my siphoning power. For the next few minutes, I was a bloodthirsty vampire, which would have been fine except for the fact that Fergus had followed me into the alley. The real vampire staggered off in one direction and Fergus took one look at the fangs protruding from my mouth and took off in another.

Unfortunately, my partner didn't run as fast as me. Fergus carried a little extra weight around the middle that slowed him down. I spent a lot of time biting my tongue when he reached for the extra donut because, gods above, I didn't want to turn into my nagging mother. Anyway, Fergus's fearful escape set off my temporary hunting instinct. Poor guy didn't stand a chance. He was one hundred percent human. He had no clue about Otherworld or the supernaturals that lived right here, hidden in plain sight.

Supernaturals like me.

I'm a rare supernatural known as a fury. Furies have been in my father's bloodline going back centuries, but the last few generations yielded only demons and magic users like witches until I came along. I got to inherit a little of everything. My siphoning power is the one that turned me fangtastic. See, I can siphon another supernatural's power—only briefly—and it leaves us both in a weakened state afterward. I can thank my mother's witchy side for that particular talent. I hate the way it makes me feel, and most of the powers possessed by other supernaturals are ones I don't want anyway. I just want to be normal, but that's not what the gods intended for me.

Thankfully, I didn't kill Fergus. The vampire traits wore off before I could do any permanent damage, but Fergus ended up in the hospital in need of a blood transfusion and the suspect got away. It was not my best day, and, unsurprisingly, it was also my last day in the field. When I arrived home that night, emotionally exhausted and racked with guilt, it got worse. I sprouted wings—huge black wings. I stood in front of the mirror for what seemed like hours, staring at the monstrous symbol of my failure with tears in my eyes. Eventually, I couldn't handle the sight of them anymore and willed them to disappear. Thankfully, they did, but they were mine now. I'd earned them by using my abilities. That was how being a fury worked. The more power you used, the more the gods gave you. Except I didn't want any of it.

I knew the job situation was bad when the Bureau ran a few tests on me and then scheduled an appointment with Dr. Suzanne Zagat, the Bureau psychiatrist. I wondered whether they were deciding to have me arrested or declared insane or both. How could I explain my abilities to a human doctor? It had been easy enough to hide my true nature through the training program. No regular human tests could detect that I was a fury. I looked and acted completely human and I'd had years of practice hiding my supernatural identity.

I sat in the waiting area of Dr. Zagat's office, pretending to read the gossip magazines on the coffee table. In truth, I couldn't focus. I was too worried about what would happen to me. I'd wanted to be an agent for as long as I could remember, my penance for the sins of my family. I'd worked so hard to be a good person and, in the snap of a fang, I'd ruined it.

The office door clicked open and Dr. Zagat's head appeared. "Come in, Agent Fury."

My stomach was harboring a hurricane. Any more movement in there and I'd hurl. Something I definitely didn't want to do under the circumstances. I stood and smoothed my shirt, trying to appear calm and completely normal.

I tripped over the threshold on the way into the office and bumped against the psychiatrist. Understandably, she jumped as though I'd attacked her.

"Sorry," I said.

"It's okay," she said, more warmly than I expected. "Try to relax. We're just going to have a nice chat."

"How's Fergus?" I had so many questions whirling inside me, but that one shot straight to the surface.

"He's absolutely fine. He's been discharged from the hospital."

Thank the gods.

She took a seat and opened the file on her desk. "Why don't you tell me exactly what happened on Thursday?"

"What does the file say?" I asked.

"I'd rather hear the story from you."

To catch me in a lie, no doubt. "The alley was dark. The suspect attacked me before running off. I was dizzy when I got up and I accidentally fell and knocked into Fergus."

Dr. Zagat cocked her head. "Fell right into his neck and accidentally lodged your absurdly pointy teeth there?"

"My mouth was open because I was yelling as I fell." An anemic excuse if I ever heard one, but it was the best I could do.

She slotted her fingers together and regarded me. "Well, you're not a vampire. So what made you choose Fergus as your next meal?"

I blinked. She just used the word 'vampire,' yet didn't seem to be freaking out, which was odd. I decided to play it cool. "I don't think this is a joking matter, Dr. Zagat."

"Apologies, you're right. Vampires aren't allowed to feed on humans, not since the Vampire Act of 1852."

I reeled back. "You really know about vampires?"

"Know about them?" she asked. "I have one for a sister-in-law." She shook her head. "Holy hell, is Madge a pain at Sunday brunch. Always insisting her Bloody Mary must be authentic or she's going home to make her own." The psychiatrist shook her head. "Yet my brother loves her. Poor sap."

I sank against the chair, instantly relaxed. "My stepmom

is a vampire." Sally. She and my father had met on one of his business trips to Otherworld.

Dr. Zagat threw back her head and laughed. "Even worse for you then."

"Not really. I don't see them often," I said. "They live back in Chipping Cheddar, Maryland, my hometown."

"Yes, Chipping Cheddar," Dr. Zagat said, her gaze dropping to the file on her desk. "And what are you then, if not a vampire?"

"I'm a fury."

Her brow lifted. "Really? The test results only say you're an MHV."

"What's an MHV?"

"It means you're of a Magical Hybrid Variety."

"The Bureau can test for that?" I asked.

"Of course. It's not part of our routine testing, but in a case like this..." She trailed off. "So, forgive me, but my knowledge of furies is a little rusty. You drive wrongdoers insane? That's your deal, right?"

"I have a lot of deals," I said.

"According to the report, your mother is a witch."

"On many levels." I paused. "Wait. You have a file on my mother?" Somehow, this news didn't surprise me.

"No, this is from the test we ran on you. Sort of like a supernatural DNA test. We also learned that your father is..." She reviewed another line. "Ah, yes, a vengeance demon. So how are you a fury?"

I shrugged. "It happens. Our last name is Fury, so they knew we had the bloodline. Then I was born and they thought they'd won the lottery, having a fury in the family. They were sure I'd be the most evil one of all." My laugh was bitter. "Boy, were they disappointed."

"Their loss is our gain." She tapped her nails on the file. "So what exactly can you do as a fury?"

5

"My powers aren't fully developed because I rarely use them," I said. I neglected to mention my shiny new set of wings.

"You stunted your own growth?"

"Basically." Much to my family's dismay. "One of my abilities is that I can siphon another's power or ability for a brief period."

"Ah, hence, your bloodlust over Fergus." She closed the file. "Now I understand. You absorbed the vampire's energy."

"Long enough to want to bite Fergus," I admitted. "Does he…remember what happened?"

"Not anymore," Dr. Zagat said. "He thinks the suspect attacked him with a knife."

"You can do that?"

She smiled. "We can do a lot of things, Agent Fury. We just keep them well hidden, just like you."

"I don't suppose the Bureau is very happy with me right now."

"You're a good agent, Eden," Dr. Zagat said. "The Bureau doesn't want to lose you. On the other hand, you've proven yourself dangerous and we can't take the risk that something like this will happen again."

"But I've been doing this job for three years and it's the first time…"

She held up a hand. "And you nearly killed your partner."

My gut twisted. I didn't want to lose this job. I'd worked too hard to get here. "I can control it. I swear."

"Or you can use it."

I opened my mouth to argue but then stopped. "You want me to use it?"

"Not here, of course. The FBI can't allow it. Too risky."

The hurricane in my stomach picked up speed. It was now a Category Five. "You're transferring me?"

She seemed pleased to finally be cutting to the chase.

"That's right. The Federal Bureau of Magic can use someone with your particular talents. San Francisco doesn't have an Otherworld portal, so there's no field office here. As it happens, though, there's an opening somewhere very familiar to you. Call it kismet." She leaned forward. "Eden, how would you like to go home?"

No, no. Not the Federal Bureau of Magic. FBM agents investigate crimes of a magical or supernatural nature in the human world. I've spent my whole life trying to distance myself from those roots. The last thing I want to do is take up the mantle in Chipping Cheddar.

My heart pounded. "No, I can't go there." Anywhere but there. "How about the portal in Antarctica? I'll go there."

"No openings there, I'm afraid. What's wrong with home?"

"I told you—my family lives there."

Dr. Zagat offered a sympathetic smile. "They can't be that bad."

Good Goddess. She had no idea. "Why is there an opening?" I asked. "What about Paul Pidcock?" The supernaturals in town tend to know each other—we were like freemasons with actual power.

Dr. Zagat pressed her lips together. "He died recently."

"Of what—boredom?" Paul was the sole agent in Chipping Cheddar for a reason. With the Otherworld portal in my hometown dormant for centuries, the FBM rarely had cases to handle in the area. Usually, it was to do with a new supernatural resident drawn to the town for its mystical energy. Someone who hadn't learned how to settle quietly among humans.

"According to the report, it was due to an unfortunate encounter with a beehive," the psychiatrist replied. "Turns out he was allergic."

Poor Paul. "I'm sorry to hear it. He was a nice guy."

"The Bureau feels that you'll be able to adequately fill his shoes, so congratulations. The position is yours."

Just like that? "And if I don't want it?"

Dr. Zagat's expression hardened. "Fergus's injuries could end up on your permanent record. That would be quite the blemish, wouldn't it? It would probably make it difficult to find work anywhere, really."

I bristled. "Why me? Why can't someone else take it?"

"Quite frankly, Agent Fury, nobody wants it. As you already know, it's boring and it's thankless. Why else would Paul Pidcock die as a result of bee stings rather than in the glory of battle?"

"The glory of battle might be overstating it slightly."

She huffed. "Work with me here, Eden. The Bureau is giving you an out. Take it."

"I guess I don't have a choice."

Dr. Zagat perked up. "I thought you'd come around. As far as people in Chipping Cheddar are concerned, you work in a field office for the cyber crimes division of the FBI, so you might want to brush up on technology terms like ransomware."

I shifted uncomfortably. "I'm not that great with computers." I barely knew how to use the filters on Snapchat.

"Who cares? It's a cover story. At least your family will still think you work for the FBI."

My family wouldn't think that. They knew all about the FBM. And they knew just enough to dance out of their reach. The long arm of the law never touched my family, not in all the years they'd lived there.

And now the long arm of the law would belong to me.

CHAPTER TWO

CHIPPING CHEDDAR IS a small town on the Chesapeake Bay in Maryland. It was settled by English Puritans with surnames like Abbot, Bradford, and Greenwood. Those that didn't turn to the water for their livelihood became dairy farmers and eventually turned their hand to cheesemaking. The town streets are still full of cheese-based names and attractive historical buildings. The closer to the bay you get, the prettier the buildings. A promenade runs along the waterfront and is popular with walkers, joggers, and cyclists. The most important thing to know about Chipping Cheddar, though, is that it houses a dormant portal to Otherworld. That's the reason the town has so many supernaturals living here. The humans don't realize it, of course, unless they possess the Sight like my childhood friend, Clara Riley. Clara is an empath, an unfortunate ability to have during our hormonal teenage years. I wondered what she'd say when she discovered I was back. I hadn't talked to her much since I moved away. As much as I liked Clara and treasured our friendship, I'd wanted a clean break from all things supernatural, or as clean as I could get when it came to my family.

I packed my car with the few belongings I owned and made the long drive to Maryland. My hellhound, Princess Buttercup, spent most of the journey with her head out the window. To supernaturals, she looked like a shaggy black monster with glowing eyes and fiery breath. To humans, she looked like a black and white Great Dane thanks to a glamour created by my mother. The witch had her uses.

I found Princess Buttercup during a trip to an oracle right before I left town for university. My older brother, Anton, had encouraged me to go and ask about my future, whether I was destined to succumb to my dark side. As a child, he tormented me with stories of black magic and violent vengeance. Anyway, I discovered the hellhound puppy abandoned outside the entrance to the underworld. I fell in love the moment I saw her and we've been a team ever since.

I pulled into the driveway of my mother's house and sat for a moment. The house looked the same as when I left. The white clapboard house with black shutters and matching front door. The wide front porch with a slightly crooked swing. It was a slice of Americana, except for the inhabitants.

My family lives on what used to be a dairy farm owned by the Wentworths, one of the Puritan families. Over time, other houses were built around theirs and eventually formed the cul-de-sac now known as Munster Close. Most of the houses are similar in nature, except the original farmhouse now occupied by my mother. Next door is Mrs. Paulson, the neighborhood busybody. She knows there's something strange about my family but she's never been able to prove it. Husbourne Crawley lives on the other side of her, a Southern transplant and white wizard partial to pale linen suits and straw hats. He's a member of the town council—the official one for humans—and serves as our supernatural mole. The three Graces also live on the close. The sisters are infuriatingly good-natured and the type of supernaturals I aspire to be. I used to visit them often as a child, trying to absorb their wholesomeness. My mother threatened to sell them to me once and I brought her my piggybank.

My father's house is a mere five hundred yards away, the result of their divorce when I was ten. They agreed to divide the expansive property and my father built a new house, where he now lived with his second wife. My mother wasn't lonely, however. She still had a full house with my grandma and Grandma's sister, my great-aunt Thora. Although I warned my mother I was coming to stay, I didn't offer any details. I figured that part could wait.

I stared at the house and sighed. "Are you ready, Buttercup?"

The hellhound barked in response. She was always ready.

I walked through the front door with the hellhound trailing behind me. She seemed to remember the house and went sniffing along the floorboards to the family room. I found my mother in the kitchen, along with Anton and my grandmother.

"Eden!" My mother dropped her spatula on the counter and bustled over to embrace me.

As my hug tightened, she wiggled away. "Careful not to crease my top, honey. I'm going out soon."

I released her and hugged my brother instead. "Good to see you."

He kissed the top of my head. "Same. I have to warn you, it's kind of a circus in here."

"Thanks to you and your children," Grandma said. "Who needs all these jars and toys? You're not raising cats." Candy, Grandma's black cat with a singularly bad attitude, was treated better than most family members.

"Verity and I are staying here while our house is being remodeled," Anton said.

"Where is Verity?" I asked. Verity is a doctor with her

11

own local practice. As a druid healer, a doctor made perfect sense as a career choice.

"Work," Anton said. "She'll be home in time for dinner. She's scaled back her hours to spend more time with the kids."

I eyed him curiously. "And why aren't you at work?"

"I was," Anton said indignantly. "I had to stop in to get my phone charger. It keeps losing battery."

"That's because you let Olivia play games on it," my mother said. "I told you that would happen."

"Wow. Olivia is playing electronic games already?" I asked. My niece was only a toddler when I left home.

"Five is still too young, in my opinion," my mother said. "It'll damage her eyes."

Anton heaved a sigh. "There's no scientific evidence that screen use will damage her eyes."

"Since when do we care about scientific evidence?" Grandma said. "We're witches."

"And Verity is a doctor," Anton stressed.

"When do I get to meet my nephew?" Ryan was only a year old, so we hadn't met in person, only an occasional video chat.

"He's napping," Grandma said. "And if you wake him, I'll kill you and bury you in the backyard next to the last person who woke him."

"Mother, stop it!" my mother said. She tucked a loose strand of hair behind her ear. "He's not the best sleeper."

"I guess Olivia is at school," I said.

"Oh, don't worry," Grandma said. "You'll know when that one comes through the door. She moves like thunder."

"She's five," I said. "How loud can she be?"

No one responded.

"So who wants to help me bring in my stuff?" I asked.

"You expect an old woman to pitch in?" My grandma

suddenly made herself appear very small and frail. It was a gift.

"Anton?" I looked at my brother expectantly.

"I would, but I have to get back to the office." He grabbed his phone charger off the counter.

"How much stuff is there?" my mother asked, suddenly concerned. "A lot?"

"I don't know. Why?" I asked. "I told you I was coming to stay. It's not my fault you didn't tell me Anton was staying here, too." With his wife and two kids, no less.

"You didn't tell me you got fired," my mother shot back.

"I didn't get fired," I huffed. "I got transferred. To here. I thought you'd be pleased."

"Pleased that you got a demotion?"

I resisted the urge to stamp my foot. "It's not a demotion. I'm in charge of the whole office here. Basically, it's a promotion."

My mother stifled a laugh. "Eden, you seem to forget that I've lived here a lot longer than you and spent a fair amount of time with Paul Pidcock."

"She's just lashing out because she has to tell everyone she works in IT instead of as a fancy field agent," Grandma said.

"It's not IT," I said.

"You told your mother computers," Grandma argued.

"Cyber crime. Computer and network intrusions," I clarified.

Grandma ignored my explanation. "Face it, Eden, you're a clout shark."

I narrowed my eyes at the elderly witch. "Have you been reading the urban dictionary again?"

Grandma shrugged her bony shoulders. "I like the internet. Passes the time."

"You know our Eden." My mother rolled her eyes. "Evil

University wasn't good enough for her. She had to go to Do-Gooder State. With *humans*."

"They have a great basketball team this year," my brother said.

"First of all, Evil University is in Otherworld and you know I had no desire to live there," I said. "Second of all, it's not called Do-Gooder State and I got a full scholarship. You should be grateful."

"Why? It would've been your student loans, not ours," my grandmother said.

No surprise that they missed the point. They didn't care about my grades when I'd earned them. They certainly weren't going to care now.

"Have you been to see your father yet?" my mother asked. I knew what her real question was—*did you see your father before you came to see me?*

"No," I said truthfully. "I figured I'd head over once I got settled here. Take Buttercup with me." Say what you want about vengeance demons, but my dad *loved* Princess Buttercup.

"I can guess why you don't want to stay with your father," Grandma said. "Starts with an S and ends with a resting bitch face."

My mother's head bobbed in agreement. "That woman sucks the energy out of your father and everyone she comes into contact with. She's an emotional vampire."

"No, Mom," I replied. "Sally is an *actual* vampire."

My mother grunted. "Whatever."

"I'll stay there if you don't have room for me," I said, knowing the riot that suggestion would incite.

"The attic isn't good enough for you?" Grandma snapped.

"The attic?" I echoed. Okay, I knew space was scarce, but I hadn't anticipated the attic.

"I'm sorry, honey," my mother said. "That's all we have available right now."

In truth, I couldn't stay with my dad even if I wanted to. My stepmom was okay as far as I was concerned, but she liked their house a certain way. If you moved the coaster an inch, there was an inquisition as to why you made that choice. I didn't need the stress, not that my mother's house was much better.

Anton sensed the tide was turning against me. He bent down and kissed my cheek. "Catch up later, okay?"

"Traitor," I hissed.

He bolted for the door before anyone could stop him.

After unloading the car, I climbed up to the attic with the first bag. It wasn't even summer yet, yet the air was already sweltering. I was going to need to shower twice a day while I stayed here. On second thought, maybe Sally's inquisitions would be worth a one-shower-per-day lifestyle.

The stacks of boxes remained untouched and there were more cobwebs than I cared to notice. I noted the mattress on the floor. At least it was covered in sheets and not dust.

"Hello, Eden."

The voice startled me and I peered into the darkness. "Alice?"

The apparition floated toward me. "It's been quite some time."

"Not for you," I said. "Probably seems like a minute has passed." Alice Wentworth is one of the many ghosts that I've encountered in Chipping Cheddar. As this farmhouse had once belonged to her family, Alice tended to hang around the property. I was the only one she could talk to—one of my abilities that I had no control over—so Alice and I had gotten to know each other pretty well during my childhood.

"I'm pleased you're back," Alice said. "It gets dull with no one to talk to and there's only so much television and web surfing a ghost can take. Your grandmother's online searches in particular are highly questionable. You should see…"

I held up a hand. "I'd rather not know, Alice."

I plopped down on the mattress. Not the most comfortable padding, but it would do for now.

"How long has my brother been living here?" I asked.

"I haven't really paid attention," Alice said. "The children are most interesting. Quite different from you as a child."

"I look forward to spending time with them."

"In that case, might I suggest you visit your father? He has the child now."

My head snapped to attention. "Wait. What? I thought Ryan was asleep."

Alice shook her transparent head. "Your father sneaks over and takes him sometimes during his naps."

"No wonder the kid has an erratic sleep schedule." What was my dad thinking?

"He's missed you greatly."

I knew Alice meant my dad. "Really?"

"He speaks to his wife about you and to Anton, of course."

"Is he still traveling a lot?" I asked. In other words, is he still carrying out his vengeance commissions?

Alice floated to the window and observed the outdoors. "Yes, but he's home now. I passed through there less than an hour ago and they were in the kitchen with Ryan."

I pulled myself to my feet. "Fine, I'll go now. Might as well rip off the Band-Aid."

"I believe Sally has baked carrot cake in honor of your return," Alice said.

I perked up. "With cream cheese frosting?"

"That I cannot say." She tapped her nose. "No sense of smell, you see."

16

"Ah, well. You had me at cake." I began to climb down the attic steps. "It's good to see you again, Alice."

"Welcome home, Eden."

"It's my little girl!" My father greeted me with a warm hug. He's the world's touchiest, feeliest vengeance demon and I both loved and resented him for it.

"Hi, Dad."

He squeezed my arms. "Who's been working out, huh? Imagine the damage you can cause with those muscles."

"I don't want to do any damage, dad, but thanks."

"Welcome back, darling." Sally crossed the kitchen to give me a cool kiss on the cheek. Unlike my father, the vampire wasn't much of a hugger.

"Did you whiten your fangs?" I asked, noticing Sally's gleaming sharp teeth. Only other supernaturals or humans with the Sight can see that Sally is a vampire. To everyone else, she looks like an attractive middle-aged woman.

"I did," Sally said. "Thank you for noticing." She gave my father a pointed look.

"Eden, have you met your adorable nephew?" my dad asked.

Ryan sat in a highchair in the kitchen. A bowl of food and a spoon were on his tray.

"Hello, Ryan," I said. "I'm your Aunt Eden. Remember me from the phone screen?"

Ryan's lips parted, revealing pink gums and a smattering of teeth.

"Who's the most evil baby in the world?" my dad said in a high-pitched voice. "You are!"

Ryan gurgled.

"Dad, he's only one. Let's not start with that already."

"Never too soon to get in touch with your true nature," he said.

"I made a carrot cake in your honor," Sally said. "Would you like a slice?"

"Yes, please," I said. I took a seat on a stool at the counter and watched Sally uncover the cake.

"Want to hear about my latest summoning?" my dad asked.

I could tell by his excited tone that I really, really didn't.

"Virgins, all of them," he said, and sliced a hand through the air.

I wanted to cover my ears. I didn't need to hear my father talking about virgins, for a summoning or any other reason.

"Nobody understands the raw power virgins have," my dad continued.

"And some of us don't want to understand," I replied.

"So a new job, Eden?" Sally asked, sensing my discomfort. She set a small plate and fork on the counter. "Must feel good to shake things up a bit. Life can get so stale."

For an immortal, maybe.

"If you wanted a new job, you should have moved into the family business," my father said.

I tried to focus on something good, like the cake. Yum. It *was* cream cheese frosting.

"I didn't want a new job," I said, my mouth full. "I liked my old job."

"You could be like your cousin Francie," my dad said, ignoring me. "*She* specializes in infectious diseases."

"Yes, in giving them to people." No thank you.

He gave me a blank look. "Well, what else?"

"Dad, you know that's not what I want out of life."

"The world needs darkness," my stepmom said. "Without it, there's no light."

18

"Sally's right," my dad said. "Someone's got to deliver the herpes hex. Might as well be you."

Sally poured me a glass of milk. "Death. Disease. It's all necessary. What's a little pestilence between friends?"

I fought to retain my composure. "I'm not the STD fairy. I'm a fury."

"Damn straight," my dad said, pounding a fist into his open palm. "Time for you to embrace it and act like one."

Inwardly, I groaned. I was home all of two seconds and my father was already trying to recruit me to the dark side. Subtle he was not.

A knock on the door saved me and I did a silent thanks to the gods. My father went to open the door and I heard the familiar voice of Mick O'Neill, the local chief of police. Mick and my dad have been friends since before I was born, although Chief O'Neill doesn't know the truth about my family. Or, if he does, he never let on.

"Eden!" Chief O'Neill exclaimed. He entered the kitchen with a big smile. "You get prettier every time I see you."

"Hi, Chief. What brings you here?" I asked. Out of the corner of my eye, I noticed Sally's fangs retract and a pop of color appeared on her cheeks.

"I'm dropping off a set of golf clubs I borrowed from your dad," Chief O'Neill said. "He always has the best toys."

"At least he's good about sharing them," I said.

"Stanley, you should know there's something strange going on with your seven iron," the chief said.

My dad's brow furrowed. "What do you mean? You broke it?"

"No, no." Chief O'Neill chuckled nervously. "Nothing like that. I had to stop using it. Every time I made contact, the ball would fly up in the air and drop straight back down where it was." He shook his head. "It was the darnedest thing."

"Hmm," my dad said. "Thanks for letting me know. I'll have it checked out."

I choked back laughter. I knew perfectly well what had happened to his seven iron. My mother delighted in using her magic to play pranks on my father ever since the divorce. Having a witch for an ex-wife wasn't easy. To be fair, having a vengeance demon for an ex-husband was no walk in the park either.

"Maybe have mom look it over," I said. "You know she has a knack for these things."

My father shot me a dark look. "Yes, she certainly does."

"I hear you're back for good," the chief said to me. "That's a surprise."

"For me, too," I said.

Chief O'Neill rubbed his hands together. "You and I might get to work together. Wouldn't that be great?"

"I'd rather she work with me," my dad said.

"As a traveling salesman?" the chief queried. "Come on, Stanley. A federal agent is pretty darn good compared to that."

"How often did you work with Paul Pidcock?" I asked.

The chief's expression clouded over at the mention of my predecessor. "What a loss to the community. Nice guy, Paul. I admit, he kept to himself and we didn't interact often, but when we did, I liked him."

Chief O'Neill is a nice guy, too. I've always liked him. I figured he kept my dad from being too evil in his daily life. Maybe I could do the same.

"Bees are a terrible way to go," Sally said with a shudder.

"Buzz," Ryan said.

"Very good!" My dad looked elated. "He's going to be a smarty. I can tell."

Chief O'Neill crossed the room to pat Ryan on the head. "He looks like Anton when Anton was this age."

I thought he looked like a smushed version of Anton with a sprinkling of Grandma thrown in, but I kept quiet.

"He eats like Anton," Sally said. "Every time I turn around, the child is hungry again. If only I could pop a vein…"

The chief laughed. "Then men could breastfeed, too."

"Yes, that's what she meant," I said hastily. My family had a tendency to speak freely, even when they shouldn't.

"Verity sends over all these bottles and jars," my dad complained. "It has to have the word 'organic' on it or we're not allowed to serve it to him. I mean, kids need to be exposed to garbage to build up their immune systems."

A horrible thought occurred to me. "You're not sneaking him actual garbage, are you?" I wouldn't put it past him. My father could be stubborn.

My father looked horrified. "Would I risk your sister-in-law's wrath?"

"Verity is…" I nearly said 'a druid' until I remembered Chief O'Neill was in the room. "Verity is not exactly known for her temper." Druids were known for their healing powers, which was the reason Verity had been drawn to a medical career. Of course, her patients often made miraculous recoveries that science could never explain. All in a day's work.

"Maybe I should take Ryan back to Mom's in case someone's looking for him," I said.

My father chuckled. "No one's looking for him. I take him all the time."

"Mom would blow a fuse if she knew."

He winked. "Why do you think I don't tell her?"

"I promise not to arrest you for kidnapping," the chief said, "but you should probably leave a note just in case someone decides to check."

"He's my grandson," my dad said. "I'll spend time with

him whenever I please. I'm certainly not stepping into *that* house to see him."

"Good thing you're home, Eden," the chief said. "Someone needs to keep an eye on this one. The older he gets, the more ornery he gets." He gave a wave. "I'll see you around. I told my deputy I'd patrol downtown so he could go to a concert."

"You're a good man, Mick," my dad said.

"Bye, Chief," I said.

He left just as my father's phone rang. The glint in his eye when he answered told me it was an Otherworld job. Chief O'Neill left in the nick of time.

"Has he been working a lot?" I asked my stepmom.

She made a face. "More than I'd like, but you know your father. He loves what he does, so he never works a day in his life."

I wish my dad didn't love exacting vengeance so much.

My father exchanged a few harsh words with the caller and hung up. "I've got to make a house call."

"Now?" Sally said. "You haven't eaten yet."

"I'll grab something on the road."

"This is why you can't lose weight," Sally admonished him. "You gravitate to junk food when you travel."

"Fine. Then I won't eat."

Sally's hands flew to her hips. "Nobody is damning anyone's soul on an empty stomach. We have standards to uphold." She opened the refrigerator.

"I'm not damning a soul today," my dad said. "My client wants revenge on a werewolf pack that keeps peeing on his lawn. He's tried wards and restraining orders, but nothing has worked."

I gaped at my father. "The whole pack?"

"You know how they are," my dad said.

Sally handed him a container of food and my father

waved his arms dramatically. "Nothing too healthy, Sally. My system can't tolerate it."

I arched an eyebrow. "What happens to your system?"

"It breaks down," he complained. "It's awful. My stomach doesn't shut up for hours."

"That's because it isn't used to healthy food," Sally replied. She pulled another small container from the shelf and handed it to him. "You can eat this on the way."

He stared at the lid. "What's in it?"

Sally's eyes formed slits. "Food."

"Just take it, Dad," I encouraged.

My father gripped the container but made it plain he wasn't happy about it. "I'd rather take the cake."

Sally kissed him on the cheek. "When you come home, dear."

My father grumbled as he left via the kitchen door.

"Men," Sally said with a shake of her head.

From his highchair, Ryan laughed and dumped his food on the floor. "Men," he said.

CHAPTER THREE

My FIRST NIGHT in the attic was fitful at best. I dreamed of Fergus and vampires and, somehow, my grandmother ended up pirouetting around the background in a ballerina costume. It wouldn't surprise me to learn that a family member had snuck a drop of potion into my evening tea to help me sleep.

My arms were stretched overhead when Anton's head appeared in the attic opening. "Are you busy?"

I yawned. "Depends on what you want. I have to get ready for work."

"Listen to this and tell me what you think."

"Is this a pitch?" Anton works in the creative department for an ad agency.

He stood in front of me and cleared his throat. "Do you have unwanted spirits in your home? Is their constant meddling starting to get you down?"

I interrupted him. "What product is that for?"

"Ghost Away," he said, and pretended to hold up a spray can.

"What about Giving Up the Ghost?" I suggested. I glanced over at Alice, hovering by the window.

"Or Ghosted," Alice said helpfully.

How did Alice know about ghosting? Nothing to do here except eavesdrop, I guess.

"Enough customers aren't going to buy that to make it viable," I told my brother.

"They will if they have a mischievous ghost."

"How about it, Alice?" I asked. "Should I splurge on a bottle of Ghost Away?"

My brother surveyed the attic. "Wow. Is Alice still here?"

"Where does he think I would go?" Alice asked, perplexed.

"She's still here," I said. "I'm the one who went away."

Anton came and sat beside me on the mattress. "How are you feeling about all that anyway? Being back?"

"It wasn't really my choice," I admitted. "You seem to be settled into your life as a family man and vengeance demon. Just like Dad."

"Not true," he said. "Dad never actually had a human world job. He just pretends to. Besides, you know I'm not into it as much as the rest of the family."

"But you don't make an effort to rail against it," I pointed out.

He gave me a blasé look. "Somebody has to bring the funk. Might as well be us."

"You don't have to. Nobody wants the funk."

"They do," he said. "There's a whole song dedicated to it. Very popular."

I smiled. "Bringing the funk is slang," I said. "It's a good thing."

"Doesn't sound very good. That's why I bring it." Anton sighed, seemingly resigned to his fate as a demon. It was a far cry from the boy who used to torture me with the kind of vengeance that only a brother was capable of. Let's just say I still check under my covers for spiders on occasion.

"Do you have a demonic side hustle?" I asked.

He gave me a pointed look. "What do you think? I have two young kids, a major home remodel happening, and I work in a creative field."

"Your wife is a doctor."

"In a small town." Anton chuckled. "Sickness doesn't pay as much as you think, not in the human world. Better to use my natural talents."

I bumped my hip against his. "Admit it, there's a part of you that enjoys it."

Anton rested his face in his hands. "There is a certain joy that comes with wreaking vengeance."

"But you're conflicted?"

"It's Verity," he admitted. "She doesn't always approve of what I do. She worries about the kids."

"Any sign of which way Ryan is leaning?" I asked. At only a year old, Ryan was too young to show signs of his nature yet. Olivia favored my brother over her druid mother, but her demonic powers were likely a watered-down version thanks to Verity's druid genes. Only time would tell.

"No sign yet," Anton said. "Dad keeps trying to coax the evil out of him."

"I noticed," I said. "We should probably try to curtail his influence."

Anton smiled to himself. "I think he forgets what it's like to have little ones around."

"I've never had little ones around, so this will be new for me."

Anton nudged me. "You were the little one."

"Mom's been messing with dad's golf clubs," I said.

He chuckled. "Better the golf clubs than his car."

"What did she do to his car?"

"Last month she put a spell on the tires to make them bounce. You should've seen Mrs. Paulson's face when he drove out of the close."

A cry from downstairs brought Anton to his feet. "That's my cue to leave."

"Leave?" I said. "Isn't that one of your kids?"

He held up a finger. "Exactly."

He disappeared from the attic before I could say another word. I decided to hurry up and get dressed so that I could head to work before anyone saddled me with a crying child.

I wasn't sure what I expected from my office, but it wasn't this. In San Francisco, my office was in a large building downtown, filled with federal employees and heavy security. Granted, I worked in the field most of the time, but I still had a decent place to sit down at a desk, fill out paperwork, and drink a decent cup of coffee.

"This can't be right." According to the information FBM headquarters gave me, my office was on Asiago Street squeezed between a tattoo parlor called Inkspiration and a donut shop called Holes.

I turned the door handle and was surprised when it opened. Not that I'd miss the daily screening to get into work, but a locked door seemed like a good idea, particularly in this part of town.

A cursory inspection revealed that the office housed two desks, a kitchenette, and a long table at the back of the room. Did Paul hold meetings here sometimes? It seemed unlikely. Who would attend?

The only window was the one at the front of the building and the blinds were drawn. I'd have to do something about the lack of natural light. I hated a dark space.

I walked over to the desk on the left and inhaled sharply.

The surface was covered with papers and not in any kind of orderly fashion. No neat stacks. Just scattered papers, Post-It notes, and slips of paper with scribbles on it. A computer hummed in the background.

The door swung open and a short, stocky guy walked in, holding a travel coffee cup. His brown hair looked as though it hadn't been combed in a week. He stopped in his tracks when he noticed me. "Oh, wow. You must be Agent Fury."

I squinted at him. "I am. Who are you?"

"Neville Wyman," he said. "I'm your assistant."

"I have an assistant?" I surveyed the quiet office. "For what?"

Neville closed the door behind him and peeked through the blinds before responding. "All your magical needs, O angry one. I'm a wizard. It's my job to create whatever you might need for a successful assignment. Charmed amulet. Cloaking spell. Paul nicknamed me Q, like in James Bond…"

"Angry one?" I interrupted.

Neville lowered his head. "Forgive me. I didn't mean to anger you, angry one. I meant it as a compliment of the highest order."

I crossed my arms and glared at him. "In what universe is that a compliment?"

"I'm told you're a fury," he explained. "One of the infernal goddesses. The Erinyes, which translates to the angry ones."

"Right." I guess it was intended as a compliment, however weird it was. "Why did Paul need an assistant to do spells for him? He was a wizard."

"He usually had other priorities," Neville said. He set the coffee cup on his desk. "I'm so sorry. If I'd realized you were coming in today, I would've gotten you one as well."

"Is it from the Daily Grind?" I asked. Just the thought of their warm, delicious lattes made my stomach yearn for one.

"No, Holes, the donut shop next door," Neville said.

"Paige is a delight. She and her husband Shia own the place, but Paige is the real backbone of the operation."

I wrinkled my nose at the prospect of drinking donut shop coffee. I'd been spoiled by San Francisco coffee shops. The Daily Grind was the only place that came close in Chipping Cheddar.

Neville took his seat, so I sat in Paul's chair. Well, my chair. "Was Paul working on anything before he died? Any cases I should know about?"

"It's been quiet of late," Neville replied. He popped the lid off his coffee and slurped. I tried not to react. Slurping was right up there with snoring and foot tapping as far as I was concerned.

"Were you close?" I asked.

Neville raked a hand through his unruly hair. "I suppose. He was often fascinated by my creations. Wanted to know my secrets so he could replicate him." Neville smiled at the memory.

I hesitated to ask my next question, but what the hell, I was nosy. "Were you with him when he died?"

Neville shook his head and took another drink. "No, but I found him."

"Oh, I'm sorry." I genuinely was. "That must've been awful."

Neville's expression grew somber. "He was due to meet me here after lunch. When he didn't turn up, I called him but got no answer, so I activated the locator charm on his phone and found him in the park down the block."

"Why was he in the park?"

"It wasn't unusual. He used it as shortcut to get here from his place." Neville shuddered. "He was covered in bee stings. He was so swollen that I barely recognized him."

"Did you know he was allergic?" I asked.

Neville nodded. "He mentioned it a couple times in passing. Wanted to know if there was a magical equivalent of epinephrine because the cost of the injectable medication had gone up exponentially."

"And is there?" I wasn't allergic to bees, but I was curious.

"Not that I could do," Neville said. "I suggested he see Dr. Verity. She's a healer." He dropped his voice to a whisper. "Druid powers."

I broke into a smile. "I'm well acquainted with Verity Fury. She's my sister-in-law."

Neville smacked his forehead. "Of course. I knew that. I'm so accustomed to calling her Dr. Verity, I forgot."

"I didn't realize she used her first name with patients," I said. I wondered whether it was a deliberate attempt to distance herself from the Fury name. It wouldn't surprise me. My family had a certain reputation in Chipping Cheddar. If you were supernatural, you steered clear because you associated them with evil and didn't want to get caught in their malevolent net. If you were human, you steered clear because they were odd. And loud. And likely to trip you if you cut in line at the supermarket. Was it any wonder I moved three thousand miles away at the first opportunity?

"Was he meeting you here after lunch to discuss a case?" I asked.

"I don't know," Neville said. "I'm not aware of one. We'd talked about organizing his desk." He inclined his head toward me. "As you can see, it's a bit of a mess."

"That's not part of your job as his assistant? To declutter the office?"

"Not really," Neville said. "Paul didn't like me to touch anything on his desk. He claimed he had a system that worked for him, but then every so often, he'd ask for my help."

"Any idea why so many bees went after him?" I asked.

"I found the hive in the park," Neville said. "It looked like he must've disturbed it as he passed and upset the occupants."

"That's too bad," I said.

Neville pressed his lips together in silent agreement.

"So what's a typical day like for us?" I asked. "Should I be reading through any files?"

"I'd start with the rules of conduct, which I have taken the liberty of dusting off for you." Neville reached into his drawer and pulled out a binder. "It's fairly comprehensive, but let me know should you have any questions."

"Thank you." I paged through the binder. "There are a lot of rules."

"Bureaucracy reigns supreme here," Neville said cheerfully. "We must preserve our secrets from the human population, all the while protecting them from creatures they're unaware of."

"Is that why our office is in the worst part of town?" I asked.

"No, that's for budgetary reasons. The Bureau doesn't earmark much money for Chipping Cheddar. With the portal here dormant, we don't have as much need as places like New York and Los Angeles."

"But the existence of the portal still draws Otherworld beings here," I said. "Chipping Cheddar's mystical energy is pretty strong for a small town."

"Agreed. And that's why we're here." He flashed a smile and I noticed a small gap between his front teeth. It was slightly endearing.

"So do you work regular hours?" I asked.

"I make them regular," Neville said. "I prefer this place to my apartment."

I glanced around the cramped office and felt a pang of sympathy for him.

Neville placed a plastic container on my desk. "Here is your FBM badge and your phone."

I stared at the two objects. "Anything special about them?"

"The FBM badge looks like a normal FBI badge to humans, but our kind can see that it's the Federal Bureau of Magic."

I held up the phone. "And this?"

"I've fitted it with a locator charm that I can activate," he said. "That's standard. My number is programmed in, as well as headquarters and the local chief of police."

I aimed it at him. "Does it also double as a gun?"

He blocked the phone and gently moved my hand aside. "No, but it has other capabilities. Wield it carefully, my infernal goddess."

"Agent Fury will do." I hoped Neville got over his shock and awe. I didn't want to be worshipped, certainly not by a guy I wasn't sleeping with. I needed a little fresh air and exercise. "I think I'll take a stroll down the promenade and drop in at The Daily Grind. Can I get you anything?"

"No, thank you," he said. "When you get back, I'll give you a demonstration of some of my inventions. I have some wonderful creations here just begging for the right opportunity."

"That sounds great," I said. I was interested to see what the FBM paid Neville to do. At this rate, I was interested to see what they paid me to do. So far, the office appeared just as sleepy as I imagined it would be. If I didn't get fresh air now, I'd be ready for a goat nap.

It wasn't the best route from Asiago Street to the promenade, but at least it meant I'd get more steps in. I tried to log my daily steps and hit at least ten thousand a day. It was easy enough in San Francisco. Lots of hilly streets.

As I walked down Roquefort Road, I admired the row of brightly painted buildings. Chipping Cheddar loved pops of color in unexpected places. In many ways, San Francisco reminded me of a bigger, better version of my hometown. Maybe that was the reason I'd subconsciously chosen it. And here I'd always thought it was because any further would land me in the Pacific Ocean.

I reached the promenade that trailed alongside the Chesapeake Bay. With the warm sunshine and gentle breeze, it was a refreshing walk. The boats beckoned me, so I decided to take a quick detour before heading for coffee. I could never live too far from water. My mother used to accuse me of having mermaid genes, as though I could choose my own DNA. If I could, I wouldn't be in this predicament right now. I'd be a normal twenty-six year old woman. One hundred percent human, with no obligation to reap vengeance or seek justice. My ancestors lived in the underworld and tortured the souls of the damned. They punished their victims by driving them mad, among other things. That's not really how I picture my life. It was no wonder my family was so infuriating. They came by it honestly. Unfortunately, I was the only one who inherited the specific fury gene.

The gentle splash of the water against the side of the promenade drew me to the water's edge. Maybe I'd spot a seal in the distance, or a selkie. Thanks to the powerful mystical energy here, supernatural water creatures were just as drawn to Chipping Cheddar as land-based beings.

I stood on the edge of the promenade and peered at the water. A smile spread across my face when I spotted a—no, wait. Not a seal at all.

Sweet Hecate.

It was a body.

CHAPTER FOUR

MY FEET REMAINED cemented to the promenade as I gaped at the body. Was it possible the person was still alive? I could swim, but I knew it would be faster to fly. I glanced around furtively and made sure no one was watching before I allowed the black wings to sprout from my back.

"Here goes nothing," I said, and vaulted over the water. I had no experience with the wings. I'd kept them hidden since the day I obtained them. It was such a short distance to the body, though, I figured I could manage it.

I figured wrong.

An unexpected gust of wind blew me off course and further away from the body.

Great balls of fury! There were boats within shouting distance. I couldn't risk being seen flying through the air. I had no choice but to extinguish the wings.

I plunged into the water and swam to the body. He was fully clothed and facedown in the water. I hooked an arm around him and used my free arm to paddle us to shore. It wasn't easy, but we made it.

I rolled him over, ready to attempt resuscitation, when I realized who it was.

Chief O'Neill.

My stomach plummeted. I did all manner of CPR in an effort to revive him, but his bloated body told me he was already dead. I stared at him in disbelief. I'd known the chief my whole life and now he was gone. How did this happen?

I pulled out my phone to call 9-1-1. After that, I dried off and sat beside the chief to wait. I took his hand and talked to him, just to keep my mind occupied. I talked about topics that would have interested him—golf, beer at the Cheese Wheel, cards with my dad. Anything to prevent my emotions from getting the best of me. I was a federal agent—I had to act like one.

Ten minutes later, help arrived—and I use the term loosely.

"Eden Fury? You've got be kidding me. I heard you were back, but I didn't believe it."

Oh, terrific.

I sprang to my feet as Deputy Sean Guthrie approached. Sean and I graduated high school together. He was the kind of kid that basked in others' discomfort and never missed an opportunity to make you feel stupid, even though he was as dumb as a sack of potatoes. It was a good thing he was all human. The last thing someone like Sean should have is power—a gun and a badge were bad enough.

"Hey, Sean." I managed what I hoped was a sad yet friendly smile. Sean was the deputy, which meant that he and I would be rubbing elbows on occasion—occasions that I hoped were few and far between.

"I thought I recognized that dark head of hair," Sean said. "It was either you or a wicked witch." He cackled at his own remark. Even as a kid, Sean seemed to be under the misguided belief that witches had black hair. Of course, his knowledge came from movies and television. He knew nothing of my family's true nature, though. He was just a moron whose jabs hit too close to home.

"At least my hair color comes with a soul," I said, drawing attention to Sean's bright red hair.

Sean made a disapproving noise at the back of his throat. "So only recently back in town and you already found a body, huh? Sounds about right."

"It's worse than you think." I stepped out of the way so that he had a better view of the deceased.

Sean's expression shifted from smug bastard to horror. "Oh my Gouda. Is that the chief?"

"I saw him in the water," I said, pointing to the spot in the bay where I noticed him. "I jumped in and dragged him to shore, but it was too late to revive him."

Sean's gaze lingered on the chief and I saw sadness reflected in his eyes. "I don't understand. How did he get in the water?"

"No idea," I said. "I'm not sure there are any witnesses either. No one was around when I came along. Only those boats in the distance." And if they didn't see me and my giant wings, it was doubtful they saw what happened to the chief.

Sean seemed frozen in place. "I can't...I don't understand how this happened."

"I'm sorry, Sean. I know you two worked closely together."

Sean kneeled down beside the chief's lifeless body. "This doesn't make sense. Why would someone murder the chief?"

I snapped to attention. "Murder? What makes you think it was murder?"

Sean twisted to look at me. "The chief never went near the water, not voluntarily. He always assigned me to the waterfront beat."

"Why?"

Sean hesitated. "He'd kill me for telling you this, but the truth is he couldn't swim."

Oh. That was surprising. "Is it possible he was out here for another reason and stumbled into the water?" I didn't want to say it out loud, but Chief O'Neill was known for his fondness for beer. He spent ample time at the Cheese Wheel in his off hours, especially following his divorce.

Sean seemed to catch on to my meaning. "We'll have the lab run tests, but I don't think so. He must've drowned early this morning." He cut a glance back at the chief. "He wouldn't be drinking that early. When he would say it's five o'clock somewhere, he meant p.m., not a.m."

"It is the breakfast of champions," I said, though I didn't really believe it myself.

Sean rose to his feet. "I'll have to catch up with you later, Eden. I have a murder to solve."

I blinked. "By yourself? At least let me help you." It wasn't like the FBM was overflowing with assignments.

"No way," Sean said. "You're not on the force. You're not even a real FBI agent. I heard you handle IT or something."

"I do not handle IT," I said.

"You do," he insisted. "You're the one who tells real FBI agents to turn their computers off and on again."

My cheeks grew warm. "I don't know where you heard that, but it isn't true." Sean would pee his pants if he knew my real job. He was oblivious to the world of vampires and werewolves.

"You don't have to be ashamed, Eden," he said. "I know you left here to be a big shot. Must be hard to come back with your tail between your legs."

If I weren't so upset about the chief, I would've clocked Sean.

"Come on, Guthrie," I said. "You're too close to this and

who knows how long it will take to bring another chief to town? You need immediate help."

"Another chief? *I* should be appointed chief," Sean said, lifting his chin a fraction. "I'm next in line."

"It's not a throne."

"I deserve to be chief," he said firmly. "Nobody knows this town better than I do."

That was unlikely, considering Sean knew nothing of the dormant portal or the supernaturals here.

"You don't have the experience to be chief," I said. "Besides, you need someone with distance to head up the investigation."

"And you would have distance?" he scoffed. "Your dad and the chief go way back." Sean pulled out his phone. "I'm in charge, Eden. Now do as I say."

I folded my arms. "Maybe you just want to get rid of me so you can destroy evidence."

He squinted at me. "Evidence of what?"

"Maybe you wanted to be chief so badly that you were willing to kill for it. You said yourself that you knew he couldn't swim. Maybe you lured him down here on purpose."

Sean reeled back. "I'm not a suspect. I would never…"

"Why not? You had motive and opportunity. I think I might have to pull out my badge and make it official." I pretended to reach for my badge.

Sean waved his hands. "Stop it, Eden. You have no jurisdiction here. You're not helping and that's final."

"He was found in the bay," I said. "Technically, that makes it the Bureau's jurisdiction." I wasn't even sure if that was true, but I knew Sean wasn't smart enough to realize that.

Sean's cheeks colored to match his hair. "That's a low blow, Eden, and exactly what I'd expect from you."

I cast a quick glance at the chief. "I'm offering to help you,

Sean. The chief of police is dead and we have no idea what happened. Two heads are better than one."

Sean kicked a stray pebble off the pavement, considering my offer. "I'll tell you what. How about we work together, at least until the new chief is named?"

"Fine with me. I only want to help, Sean. Chief O'Neill was a family friend. My dad is going to be devastated." And I had no idea how he'd react to news that his good friend was murdered. Scratch that—I knew exactly how he'd react. He'd want to run out the door and hunt the culprit down to exact revenge. I had to make sure I got involved to prevent any shenanigans from the supernaturals in town.

Sean stared at the chief's lifeless body. "I'm sure we can work together in the chief's honor, but I'm the one calling the shots."

"Sure you are, Sean. I wouldn't dream of undermining your authority." I didn't bother to cross my fingers behind my back. There was no way Sean could believe I meant any part of that statement. We'd known each other too long.

Sean extended a hand. "Deal?"

I decided to shake it. I'd wash off the ginger cooties later. "Deal."

After I broke the news of the chief's death to my family, I felt compelled to seek out Clara Riley. I had an overwhelming urge to apologize for the way I'd treated her. There's nothing like the death of someone you know well to make you think hard about past choices, and I'd definitely made a poor choice concerning Clara. I knew she'd be less than thrilled to see me. We'd been joined at the hip from kindergarten until I left for college. Since then, our communications slowed dramatically, mainly because I was trying to wedge a gap between Chipping Cheddar and me. Although it wasn't fair to Clara, I'd believed I was doing what I could to protect myself from my evil inclinations. A lot of good it did me in the end because here I was, back in Chipping Cheddar. After the day I'd had, I figured I could take whatever she dished out. I deserved it.

I asked Aunt Thora to do a locator spell using a photo Clara had given me before I moved away. I'd kept it on my dresser in San Francisco and it was on a pedestal table in the attic now. The spell pinpointed Clara's location. She was at the Gouda Nuff diner over on Pecorino Place.

It only took ten minutes to drive and park. Downtown was rarely jammed with cars. It was the pedestrians you had to watch out for. They had a tendency to forget that cars existed in Chipping Cheddar, until one ran over their toes.

I stopped in front of the diner, mentally preparing myself for the reunion. Would she ignore me? Throw a drink in my face? No, not Clara, though I deserved it.

When I glanced in the double bay window, I was shocked to see Clara in a booth, laughing with Sassafras Persimmons. 'Sassy,' as she was known by locals, was our nemesis in high school. The blond cheerleader delighted in making everyone's lives a misery around her, especially ours. As an empath, Clara couldn't handle too much misery. Sassy was also forever making moves on my boyfriend at the time, Tanner Hughes. One move eventually worked our senior year because I found them together in a compromising situation on prom night. It had taken all my strength not to go full fury on them, not that they would have known what I was capable of. They were both human. Clara was, too, except as an empath, she possessed the Sight. She knew all my family's secrets and had kept them, even after we drifted apart. Although seeing her now with Sassy, I wondered whether my secrets were safe after all.

Before I had a chance to escape, the two left the diner and

Sassy practically bowled me over on the pavement. With her silky hair and perfect complexion, Sassy didn't appear to have aged a day and she wasn't even a vampire. Completely unfair. Clara looked good, too. Her light brown hair was pulled back in a low ponytail and, thanks to time in the sun, she'd gained a few new freckles across the bridge of her nose.

"Eden Fury? Are you serious?" Sassy's eyes blazed with annoyance.

"I have every right to breathe oxygen in this town, Sassy, same as you." My gaze shifted to my former best friend. "Hi, Clara. I was coming to find you."

Clara's expression was inscrutable. "Why?"

"To tell you I was here," I said, feeling awkward.

"You have my number," she said pointedly. "You could have called."

She wasn't going to make this easy on me, nor should she. I'd been a horrible friend and she deserved better. Not that I'd describe Sassy Persimmons as better. If Sassy had been a witch, I might be convinced she'd spelled Clara to be her friend.

"I thought it would be best to talk in person," I said.

"So you're home for a visit? What happened?" Clara asked, her tone sprinkled with a touch of bitterness. "Did someone die?"

"Actually, someone did," I replied. I told them about Chief O'Neill. Anything to distract from the current awkwardness.

"That's awful," Clara said. Her expression softened and I was relieved to see that the empath was alive and well in there. For all I knew, Sassy could've driven it out of her. "I can't believe Cal hasn't called to tell me. This is big news."

"He probably has Gasper covering it," Sassy said.

"Cal?" I queried. "You mean Calybute Danforth?" Cal Danforth owned the local newspaper, *The Buttermilk Bugle*.

"That's right," Clara said. "I'm a reporter there. Sassy works there, too."

Well, that explained the inexplicable friendship. "You're a reporter, Sassy?"

"I sell advertising," Sassy clarified.

Now that made more sense to me. I could imagine the local shop owners—the men, at least--falling all over themselves to give Sassy their business.

"The chief wasn't very good at his job if he let himself get murdered," Sassy said.

"Yes, I'm sure he fully cooperated with someone pushing him into the bay," I said.

"Chief O'Neill was a wonderful chief of police," Clara said. "Are we sure it was murder? Maybe it was an accident?"

"It's possible," I said, but, based on Sean's reaction, I doubted it. The chief wasn't clumsy and his love of food didn't seem to throw off his equilibrium.

"Do you think Sean will become the new chief?" Sassy asked. "Can you imagine?" She tossed her blond locks over her shoulder. "If I wasn't already dating the hottest guy in town, I might consider taking on the chief of police."

"He must be new in town then," I said. "Otherwise, he'd know which women to avoid."

Sassy's lips curved into a malevolent smile. "Tanner never wanted to avoid me. In fact, he can't get enough of me. Never could."

A lump formed in my throat, though I couldn't imagine why. Tanner Hughes was old news. There had been several guys since him. Well, maybe not several but…Okay, there'd been no one since Tanner.

I glanced at her hand. "No ring, huh? Maybe he's had enough, but you haven't gotten the memo yet." Kind of like what happened to me.

Sassy scowled. "We're still young. There's no rush." She brushed past me. "Come on, Clara."

I met Clara's uncertain gaze. "Want to stay and have a coffee with me? Play catch-up?"

Clara looked from me to Sassy. "Maybe another time."

"That's her nice way of saying see you in Hell," Sassy said.

"You realize that means she'd be there, too," I pointed out. "Do you think Clara is going to Hell?"

Sassy appeared momentarily confused. She wasn't the sharpest bristle on the broom.

"It's okay, Sassy," Clara said, patting her friend's back. "I knew what you meant." Clara glanced at me. "You should go see your dad. He'll be upset about the chief."

"When he comes home," I said. "He's working."

Clara lowered her gaze. She knew what that meant.

I watched them walk away, and a great sadness swept over me. I hadn't considered what it would be like to see Clara again. I didn't blame her for making new friends, although why she'd choose Sassy was beyond me.

Clara was right about my dad, but I left it to Sally to break the news when he arrived home. She was his wife and the best one for the task.

I considered returning to the office, but I was too depressed. I turned on my heel and headed back to the car to drive home.

CHAPTER FIVE

My family made it difficult to focus on my grief over the chief and Clara, which was probably a good thing.

The doorbell rang, giving me an excuse to walk away from the cacophony in the kitchen. Between the children, the animals, and the loud adults in the family, it was a wonder Alice didn't decide to haunt another house.

I was shocked to see my father on the front porch. "You rang the bell?"

He shrugged and stepped inside. "Not my house anymore."

He trailed behind me into the open-plan kitchen and everyone stopped talking when they spotted him.

"Stanley," my mother said tersely.

My father gave a curt nod. "Beatrice."

No one else breathed a word, interested to hear what my father had to say.

"A bunch of people are going to the Cheese Wheel tonight in honor of Mick," he announced. "I think we should all go and pay our respects."

"All of us?" I queried. I shot a quizzical glance at my

mother. She and my father were reluctant to share oxygen at the best of times. The chief's death certainly didn't qualify.

"I think that's a marvelous idea," my mom said. "Let me freshen up and Eden and I will meet you over there."

"What about me?" Anton asked. "I liked the chief."

"Your wife is working late. That means you have important duties here," my mom said. She inclined her head toward Olivia, who sat quietly on the couch paging through a picture book. Upon closer inspection, I saw that it was titled *The Little Demon That Could*. A gift from Otherworld, no doubt.

"Aunt Thora will be here," Anton said. I noted that he failed to mention Grandma.

"Aunt Thora is in bed already," my mother replied. "She's not active enough to handle your feisty children."

"Ryan's already in bed," Anton said.

"I'll put the little demon to bed," Grandma said, appearing out of nowhere.

Anton shifted uneasily. "On second thought, I think I'd like to be here when Verity gets home. Give her a nice foot massage."

Grandma slid her foot out of her slipper. "You can practice on me until she gets home. I've got a bunion that won't quit."

Anton grimaced. "That's what magic is for."

"Sally and I will meet you over there," my father said. Apparently, he didn't want to see Grandma's bunion either.

"Grandma, put your slipper back on," I said. "You're frightening Olivia." I'd noticed my niece was fixated on her great-grandmother's bare foot.

"I'm not frightened," Olivia said matter-of-factly. "I'm merely curious. Mommy says the human body is nothing to be ashamed of."

"I'm not ashamed," Grandma said. "I'll show you." She began to untie the belt on her robe.

"Grandma," I said sharply.

"You need to loosen up, Eden," she told me. "Maybe have a drink before you go out to drink."

"I don't need to drink to loosen up," I countered. "I'm a very relaxed individual."

Everyone stifled a laugh and my mother hurried away to fix her face, or whatever she did in the bathroom for excessive periods of time.

"What?" I asked. "It's true."

"Prove it," Grandma said. "Have a glass of one of your aunt's lemon sours."

Aunt Thora's homemade lemon sour? "No need to twist my arm." It was like nectar from the gods and I knew this because Anton and I had pilfered some from the liquor cabinet when we were teenagers. Anton drank so much that he...

"We agreed we'd never mention that again," Anton said, interrupting my thoughts. He wasn't psychic, but he often seemed to know what I was thinking. Genetics at work.

"You can risk a glass," I said. "Grandma keeps adult diapers in her closet if you need to borrow one."

I expected to incur the wrath of both of them. Instead, my grandmother was strangely quiet. "Let me get that drink for you. You don't want to miss out on the festivities like your brother here."

"Auntie Eden, will you read this to me?" Olivia held up a different book than the one she had earlier.

I moved closer to read the title.

Grandma handed me a glass filled with lemony goodness. It slid right down my throat and warmed my belly.

"Now that is a perfect drink," I said. I handed the empty glass to Grandma.

"I'm glad you think so."

"Aren't you going to have any?" I asked.

"What makes you think I haven't already?"

"Let's go, Eden." My mother emerged from her bedroom, fluffed and folded. She stopped short when she saw me. "You haven't changed."

"I never said I was going to."

"That's her way of saying 'is that what you're wearing?'" Anton said.

"I speak Mother fluently, thanks," I said. "And both of those statements are passive aggressive."

"It's just that the Cheese Wheel will be full of eligible young men," my mother said.

"What is this, Jane Austen?" Grandma griped. "She moved home two seconds ago. You don't need to marry her off to the first drunken bozo she bumps into."

"Thank you, Grandma," I said.

"I mean, that's how you ended up married to Stanley Fury," Grandma continued. "We don't need history to repeat itself."

My mother turned and stomped toward the front door. "Come along, Eden."

I grabbed my handbag and followed her to the car.

Unfortunately, the first people I saw when I entered the bar were Clara and Sassy. Sassy was flirting with two guys in muscle shirts and Clara looked bored out of her mind. I couldn't resist a smile.

"Go and talk to Clara, honey," my mom said. "I'll be mingling over there." She waved a hand in the air.

"Eden, I didn't think you'd come tonight," Clara said, as I approached.

"It was Dad's idea."

"Here, I'll buy you a drink," she offered.

"Don't be silly," I said. "I'm the one who should be buying

you a drink after the way I behaved." I started to maneuver my way to the bar, but the room was thick with people.

"Hold on," Clara said. "Tell me what you want and I'll have Sassy get it. She's an expert."

I'll bet. "I'll have a Cheddar Fizz."

Clara smiled. "Missed the house specialty, did you?" She tapped Sassy on the shoulder and whispered in her ear.

"Excuse me, fellas," Sassy cooed. "I need to order a round of Cheddar Fizz."

"Oh, let me get those for you," the beefy guy said. "Three?"

"That's so sweet of you," Sassy said. She touched his arm.

"I thought she was with Tanner," I whispered to Clara.

"He's out of town until tomorrow morning," Clara said.

No sooner did I have a drink in hand than a ghost came rushing toward me. Okay, not an actual ghost like Alice, but much, much scarier.

Tanner's mother--Gale Hughes.

I sucked down the drink as fast as I could.

"I thought that was your black head darkening our doorstep, Eden Fury," she said. She somehow managed to sound racist about my hair color. "What happened? Relationship gone bad so you cut and run...again?"

The 'again' dangled between us. She was baiting me and I wasn't going to give her the satisfaction of biting. Tanner's mother was under the delusion that her son walked on water and, thus, was permitted to walk all over everyone in his path.

"I got a promotion," I lied. What was a little white lie between enemies?

Gale frowned. "A promotion brought you back home? What kind of job considers Chipping Cheddar a step up?"

"Hey," Clara interjected. "This is a great town."

Gale brushed past me to kiss Sassy's cheek. "Hello, daughter." The men Sassy had been flirting with eased away with

Gale's appearance. Older woman repellant. Worked every time.

"Not daughter yet," Sassy said brightly. "Maybe this year, though."

Gale pinched her cheek. "Patience is a virtue. A guy like Tanner only comes along once in a lifetime." She tossed me a haughty look over her shoulder. "Sometimes it bears remembering."

I found it ironic that Gale cared so much about our breakup when she never wanted me to date Tanner in the first place. She disliked my whole family, and had made it clear from our first date that she didn't approve. She thought Tanner was a gift from the gods and that he deserved better than 'that strange Fury girl.' Sassy made more sense. The blond cheerleader and all-around bitch was right up his alley.

Gale maneuvered past us to speak to a woman I didn't recognize. I noticed Sassy's relieved expression.

"You don't care for her?" I queried.

Sassy bit her lip, clearly debating whether to confess this perceived sin of disliking her future mother-in-law. "She can be a bit much, you know?"

I knew all about 'a bit much' in my house. "She's not so bad if you compliment her. She soaks it up like my father soaks up..." I nearly said 'rev-energy,' but I caught myself. Rev-energy is the term we use to describe the energy he absorbs from the revenge he inflicts on his victims.

"The sun," Clara finished for me. "He's a total sun worshipper."

I offered a grateful smile. "Anyway, Gale likes you a lot better than she ever liked me, so you've got that in your favor."

Sassy visibly relaxed. "Another drink, Eden?"

I emptied my glass and set it on the bar. "Sure. Why not?" I was already feeling the effects of the first drink, which was surprising. I figured it was just the intense atmosphere. Too many blasts from the pasts.

The next thing I knew, my father was standing on a table and demanding that everyone raise their glasses in honor of the chief.

"To the chief," everyone said in unison and drank.

The music quieted so that people could tell stories about Chief O'Neill. The time he saved a cat from a tree. The time he drove around town in his cop car with a little boy suffering from cancer. The ride had been the boy's dying wish.

"Where's Sean?" Sassy asked, scanning the crowd.

"I'm sure he's on duty until a new chief arrives," I said.

"Sean would make an awesome chief," Sassy said.

"A potato would make a better chief than Sean," I shot back. To my surprise, both girls laughed.

"You're fun when you're drinking," Sassy said. "You should do that more often."

"You're fun when you're not being a complete tart. You should try that more often."

Sassy smiled. "How about another round?"

"Or better yet," I said. "Shots!"

Clara gave me a funny look but said nothing. I bought a round of tequila shots and we downed them before Clara and Sassy decided they needed the restroom. My bladder was as supernatural as the rest of me. I could go for hours without needing to pee, and, for some reason, decided to share that last bit with Sassy.

She laughed as the two of them disappeared down the narrow corridor.

I stood beside the bar and ordered another drink while I waited for them to come back. I assumed Sassy was taking the opportunity to unload on Clara about me. It was fine with me. I'd do the same later--who cares if it was to Alice? Ghosts were excellent listeners.

My head was slightly dizzy and I wondered whether I should slow down. Then again, I was fun, according to Sassy. I liked being fun. It made me feel—normal.

"Excuse me. Are you Eden?"

I turned to see a gorgeous guy in a uniform towering over me. He had to be at least six foot three. My legs went numb at the sight of his sea-green eyes and square jaw. Even through the stubble, I glimpsed a dimpled chin.

I choked up as I attempted to answer. "I'm Eden," I croaked.

"I'm Chief Fox," he began, and I started to laugh.

"Fox? Oh, nice one," I said. "Who put you up to this? Sassy?" They probably lied about going to the restroom. It was all a ruse to play a joke on me.

He squinted. "Who's Sassy?"

"No, I bet it was my grandmother." She accused me of being uptight earlier. Chief Fox was likely her way of trying to loosen me up. I wagged a finger. "Whoever it was, tell them they can't fool me. I'm a federal agent." I tapped the side of my head. "That makes me smart."

He tilted his head, seemingly perplexed. "Fool you? In what way?"

I stuck my finger in his dimple and gave him a gentle push. "You're probably naked under those clothes."

He grinned. "That's basically how clothes work."

"Ha-ha," I said. "How long before you take them off?"

"Excuse me?" Chief Fox, or whatever his real name was, pretended to be taken aback by my question.

"You've got an innocent face, Foxy. I'll give you that much." I patted his cheek. "Those eyes, though." I sucked down the rest of my drink. "Everything I see there is dirty, dirty."

His dirty eyes twinkled with amusement. "I think I chose my moment unwisely. It's just that I heard you were here and you're on my list of people to meet."

"Oh, I bet." I looked him up and down. "Just out of curiosity, how long is your so-called list?" I placed my palm flat against his chest. "No, wait. Don't tell me. You can show me later." I winked at him.

"I think it's best if we postpone this conversation," he said.

"Eager to get to the good stuff first, huh?" I reached up to unbutton the top button of his shirt. "I bet those abs deserve a badge of their own." My fingers stopped when I noticed his actual badge glimmering under the artificial lights. "That's a pretty realistic badge, Foxy. Looks just like the chief's." I sighed dramatically. "Such a good man. He will be missed."

"I understand that's why the bar is so packed tonight," he said. "Looks like half the town came out to celebrate his life."

"Eden?" Clara returned to my side. "What are you doing?"

I looked at her and smiled. "Playing with my new toy. Isn't he pretty?" I grabbed Foxy's face and squeezed his cheeks. "Not too shabby waking up to this every day, is it?"

Clara frowned. "Um, Eden…"

Sassy emerged from behind Clara. "I think she wants you to cuff her, Chief."

Foxy gently removed my hand from his face. "As long as she's not driving home, I think I'll leave her be."

"Leave me be?" I slurred. "Not much of a stripper then, are you?"

Sassy began to laugh hysterically. "Oh, this is a dream come true. Please keep talking."

Clara slipped an arm around my waist. "Eden, this is the new chief. Sawyer Fox."

"You're so funny, Clara," I said. "Has anyone ever told you that?" I leaned my head on her shoulder. "I've missed my best friend."

Foxy stuck out his hand. "Chief Sawyer Fox. It's nice to meet you, Agent Fury."

I stared at him, unblinking. My head remained on Clara's shoulder, which was starting to trigger a cramp in the curve of my neck. "Who told you I was an agent?"

"Well, you did, but I already knew. I've been getting up to speed on everyone in town I should speak to," he replied. "I thought the Cheese Wheel would be a nice icebreaker." He paused, his gaze lingering on me. "Which arguably it has been."

Slowly, I lifted my head. "So you're...not a stripper?" A burp escaped me and I covered my mouth, mortified.

"Only when it's time for bed," he said, plainly amused.

My brain struggled to make sense of the situation. "Then why do you look like an underwear model?" He looked like a guy who liked to do push-ups on his paddleboard while out in the bay.

"Do I?"

I faced Clara. "I don't feel very well."

"How about I take you home?" Clara asked.

"Seriously?" Sassy demanded. "She's back in town for two seconds and already ruining our fun?"

Chief Fox took one look at Sassy's pinched face and turned back to me. "It was a mistake to come here tonight, I can see that now. I'd be happy to escort Eden home."

"Oh, we'll take care of her..." Clara objected.

"No, really. It's no trouble," he said. "My car is right outside. I've got the flashing lights and everything."

I was too tired and unwell to object.

Clara removed her arm from around my waist, not realizing she was the only thing holding me up. I immediately plunged to the floor.

CHAPTER SIX

I WOKE up the next morning with a pounding headache. No surprise there.

"You look absolutely terrible," Alice said, hovering over me. "Is it the pox?"

"It's not the pox," I mumbled. My mouth was too dry to speak properly.

"You overindulged?"

"Apparently." I struggled to sit up and the room tilted. I fell flat again. My body wasn't ready to face this day.

"Who's Chief Fox?" Alice asked. "Is he the replacement for Chief O'Neill?"

I pulled the covers over my face as last night's events came flooding back to me. Dear gods. I only just moved back and now I'd have to leave town again. Forever.

I flipped down the covers. "How did you hear about him?"

"Your mother and grandmother were talking in the kitchen this morning. They said he carried you out of the Cheese Wheel and into his police cruiser. According to your mother, it looked like the final scene from *An Officer and a*

Gentleman, except you were waving around an empty cocktail glass instead of a factory cap."

I wanted to die. How did I get so drunk on cheap cocktails? They weren't anything special. The Cheese Wheel was known for its weak drinks.

I peered at Alice. "Did you hear them say anything else…about me?"

"They said that, by the end of the night, your hair looked like you'd been caught in an electrical storm in the Grand Canyon."

Lovely. "Anything else?"

"They said Chief Fox was delicious." She paused. "I never really understood that way of describing someone you find attractive. Modern language has taken quite the turn since my time."

I was inclined to agree—he *was* delicious. A memory sharpened in my mind. My fingers attempting to open the chief's shirt.

"Sweet Hecate," I said. I turned to the side and puked—straight into a bucket. "How did that get there?"

"Your mother brought it up this morning," Alice said. "She seemed to think you'd need it when you awoke."

She either thought I was drunk enough to vomit or she knew that I'd been spelled, most likely because she or Grandma was the witch responsible. I rolled off the mattress and climbed downstairs to confront the guilty party. I took a detour at the bathroom to brush my teeth because I couldn't stand the lingering taste of last night on my tongue.

I found my mother in the kitchen with Grandma and Aunt Thora. My mother had just removed a hot pan from the oven and placed it on the stovetop. The smell of fresh banana bread was usually a welcome one, but right now I wanted to run back to the bathroom.

"Good morning, Eden. How are you feeling?" Verity stood in front of Ryan's highchair, trying to spoon-feed him.

"Not great," I said. I gave my mother a pointed look.

"That's too bad," my mother said. "Looks like someone had a good time last night."

"I heard you gave the new chief a lap dance," Grandma said.

I folded my arms. "I did no such thing." I paused and looked at my mother. "Did I?"

"No," my mother said. "But I would've paid good money to see that."

"I would've recorded it on my phone and uploaded it to YouTube," Grandma added.

"Esther, don't be cruel," Aunt Thora chastised her.

"That ship sailed before I was born," I said.

"Stupidity is what happens when you've had a skinful before nine o'clock," Grandma said.

"A skinful?" Verity echoed.

I groaned. "It means enough alcohol to make me drunk."

Verity understood. "Ah. Urban dictionary again?"

I gave her a thumbs up.

"I can give you something for the nausea," Verity offered. "Grandma, would you mind taking over Ryan's feeding?"

"I don't see why the kid can't feed himself yet," Grandma grumbled. Still, she took the spoon from Verity and held it a few inches from Ryan's mouth. "Can you say diabolical?"

"Of course he can't," Verity said. She rifled through the cabinet and retrieved a packet of powder. "Mix this with cold water."

"Is it a druid mixture?" I asked.

"It's one of my specialties," Verity said. "Your brother's needed it on more than one occasion." She cast a knowing glance over her shoulder in the direction of my mother. "When the situation warranted it."

"Why are you looking at me?" My mother was the picture of innocence.

"Because you spelled me last night," I said. "Admit it."

"I admit no such thing," my mother said. She transferred the bread to a cooling rack. It was a perfect loaf. Then again, she'd always preferred baking to mothering. She had more control over the ingredients.

Verity mixed the powder in a cup of cold water and handed it to me. "This should fix you up."

"Thanks, but will it fix what happened with the new chief?" I asked. I downed the concoction and was pleased to note that it tasted slightly minty.

"That's on you," Grandma said. "If you weren't hell-bent on making a fool of yourself, you wouldn't be in this predicament."

I rounded on her. "Where do you get the idea that I'm hell-bent on making a fool of myself?"

"You always have been." Grandma shoved another spoonful of food into Ryan's mouth before he could object. "Dating that no-good human..."

"Tanner?" I asked. My voice went a few octaves higher than intended at the mention of my cheating high school boyfriend.

"Speaking of Tanner, why on earth were you socializing with Sassafras Persimmons last night?" my mother asked.

Hmm. It hadn't occurred to me that a benefit of befriending Sassy would be annoying my family. Suddenly, more time with the bitchy blonde seemed like a good idea.

"That girl's had more lays than a potato chip bag," Grandma said.

"Grandma!" Verity said. "Olivia is right in the family room on the sofa."

"What's a lay?" Olivia called from the adjacent room.

"What hens do," Verity replied smoothly. "It's about eggs."

"And ovaries," Grandma added.

"Esther, that's enough," Aunt Thora said softly.

My grandmother's sister was often the only one who could get through to her. It was a blessing that she lived here.

"If you don't like what I have to say, you can always move out," Grandma told Verity. She grabbed a cloth and wiped Ryan's messy face.

"No one is moving out," my mother said. "Not until it's time."

"These kids are noisy," Grandma said.

"You're the noisiest one in this house," Verity shot back. The color immediately drained from her face and I knew she was regretting opening her mouth. Although Grandma was unlikely to seek revenge on Verity, she'd be more than willing to retaliate against my brother. Last night was bad, but I knew they were capable of a lot worse. When I was fifteen, Grandma spelled me so that every time I tried to say something nice, I burped instead. They'd been trying to beat the good out of me for a long time.

"I told everyone the chief looked young," Aunt Thora said, deftly changing the subject. "I ran into him when I was leaving the hair salon yesterday. He was very friendly." She cut a lemon and dropped a slice into her water.

"I don't think he's a day over thirty," I said.

"And he's hot," my mother chimed in. "His looks suggest more TV cop that reads scripted lines than actual chief of police with investigative skills."

"That's offensive," Grandma said.

"To whom?" my mother asked.

"To attractive people like me," Grandma said. "I'm living proof that you can be good-looking and ridiculously intelligent."

I groaned. "Or just ridiculous."

"What?" Grandma said, shaking the dirty spoon at me.

"You should be grateful you favor me and not your father's side of the family."

"Grandma's right," my mother said. "Chief Fox wouldn't have been eyeing you the way he did if you looked like your father."

I hesitated. "He was eyeing me?" Likely because I was a drunken idiot who'd mistaken him for a stripper.

"Like Moyer eyed that tiara during the gay pride parade," Grandma said.

"How is Uncle Moyer?" I asked.

"Find out for yourself by stopping by," Grandma replied. "It'll give Tomas a five-minute break from talking about himself."

"Don't speak ill of my son-in-law," Aunt Thora said. "Tomas is lovely."

"For an angel hybrid," Grandma replied. She'd never forgiven her demon nephew for marrying a human-angel hybrid. Tomas is no typical angel, though. His human tendencies tend to be in control most of the time—well, the vices anyway.

"I'm going to shower," I said. "I reek of the Cheese Wheel."

"More like desperation from the way you were throwing yourself at the new chief." Grandma dropped the spoon into the sink and sniffed the freshly baked loaf of bread. "You didn't add enough cinnamon."

"Of course I did," my mother said, appalled by the suggestion.

I took the opportunity to escape during their argument. It was like letting the T-Rex tangle with the Velociraptors at the end of the original Jurassic Park. No need for me to stick around and witness the resulting carnage.

By the time I showered and dressed, I felt more like myself again, thanks to Verity's cure. I still wasn't sure which spell had been inflicted upon me, but at least it was over now. If only the damage were, too.

I debated whether to try to make peace with the chief or pretend last night never happened. Chances were good that I'd be crossing paths with him on a semi-regular basis. It was probably best to take the high road.

"Has anyone seen Princess Buttercup?" I asked, returning to the kitchen on my way out.

"She was in the garden earlier," Aunt Thora said. She glanced up from the cookbook she was reading at the table. "She loves the morning sunlight."

"Would you make sure she doesn't leave the property?" I asked. "I don't want to freak out any of the neighbors."

"The humans won't see her for what she is, honey," my mother said.

"Still, a huge Great Dane running around the cul-de-sac might still unsettle a few people," I said. Like Mrs. Paulson.

"Not to worry, I'll keep an eye on her," Aunt Thora said.

"Thank you. You're the best."

As I sailed out the door, I heard my grandmother say, "No, I think you'll find *I'm* the best."

I drove through the residential section until I hit Feta Way and then took that into downtown. I snagged a spot on Pecorino Place and was feeling mighty proud of myself for about two seconds before my luck changed right in the middle of Pimento Plaza.

"Wow. Eden, you're really back."

My heart thumped wildly in my chest at the sound of his voice and I was sure that even the statue of Arthur Davenport, one of the town founders, could hear it.

Slowly, I turned to face him. "Hey, Tanner. It's been a long time." Not long enough. He looked the same. Maybe ten pounds heavier, which in his case was a good thing. He'd been long and lanky in high school and now he was more filled out.

He observed me from head to toe and a slow smile emerged. "A few years away and you come back looking like a rock star."

I glanced down at my jeans and light purple top. Rock star's casual accountant, maybe, but not rock star. "Um, thanks. I was out with Sassy and Clara last night." I waited to gauge his reaction.

His smile didn't waver. "Yeah, she told me about your drunken run-in with the new chief. Sorry I missed it, but I was out of town. I travel a lot for work." He wiggled his eyebrows. "I'm an international man of mystery now."

"You sell medical equipment in the Mid-Atlantic region."

His smile faded. "I guess you and Sassy did some catching up."

"We did." And it wasn't as terrible as I'd feared, not that I would tell Tanner. He'd likely take it as an invitation for a three-way.

"I never stopped thinking about you, you know," Tanner said. "After we broke up and you left town." He pinned his soulful gaze on me and I pushed away the butterflies in my stomach. The physical response was nothing more than a habit, like muscle memory. I wasn't even attracted to Tanner, not anymore.

A hand shifted to my hip. "Were you thinking about me when you were with Sassy? Because that's horribly disre-spectful—to both of us."

Tanner offered a playful smile. "You're still upset about that? It was so long ago."

"You're dating Sassy now," I said. "If you never stopped thinking about me...Well, you do the math."

Tanner's brow furrowed. "What kind of math?"

I'd forgotten how dim Tanner was. "It was a pleasure

running into you. Now if you'll excuse me, I have work to do."

He latched onto my arm as I tried to walk away. "I hear you're a big time FBI agent now. That's pretty cool. I always knew you were destined for greatness."

Any further up my derriere and he'd be examining my tonsils. "I live here now, Tanner. We have plenty of time to take a stroll down memory lane."

"And hopefully make new ones." He tried to fix me with that soulful look again, but I dodged his gaze. At least I knew he was same old Tanner. No need for a second chance, not that I would've considered it. It would've driven my family crazy, which was a huge bonus, but it wasn't worth it to me.

"See you around," I said. I continued to the police station where I hoped to find Chief Fox so I could get my apology out of the way and restore my dignity.

I stopped in front of the secretary's desk and was surprised to see that Judith Stanton still worked here. The woman had to be pushing eighty.

"Mrs. Stanton, do you remember me?"

Judith peered at me from behind oversized glasses with gold trim. They were pretty fancy for the eighty-year-old secretary at the police station.

"The Fury girl. Edith."

"Eden," I said.

"Right. That's what I said." She shook her head in annoyance.

"I'd like to see the chief if he's available," I said.

"Chief O'Neill isn't here. He's dead." She clucked her tongue. "Such a tragedy when they're taken from us so young."

I wanted to point out that Chief O'Neill wasn't *that* young, but I decided to bite my tongue. "I mean the new chief. Sawyer Fox."

Judith appeared momentarily confused. "Oh, the hot guy. Yeah, he's in there." She jabbed a thumb over her shoulder. "I'll let him know you're here." She paused. "Why are you here?"

"Official business," I said, and walked straight through the open doorway of the chief's office.

Sawyer Fox sat at his desk, reviewing a file. He glanced up when he heard my footsteps. "It's only ten and my day's looking up."

Why did he have to look gorgeous when I was sober and spell-free? I was hoping last night's view of him was the result of magic or cocktail vision.

"Hello Chief Foxy." I halted mid-step, my cheeks burning. "I mean, Fox. Chief Fox." What was wrong with me? Did my mother slip something into Verity's powder?

Chief Fox grinned. "I hope you brought a roll of ones for my G-string. You owe me from last night."

I opened my mouth but no words came out. This wasn't how I expected my apology to go.

"I'm sorry," he said. "That wasn't very professional of me."

I held up a hand. "That's okay. I deserve it. Last night was not my best moment."

He chuckled. "Well, it seemed like a pretty good one from where I was standing."

"I'd had a few drinks…"

"You don't say." His smile was having an effect on me—and by effect, I mean I felt compelled to throw myself across his desk and ask to see his G-string.

"It's my fault, really. I should have realized people would be drinking in honor of Chief O'Neill. I shouldn't have come in uniform and expected to conduct police business. It was poor judgment."

"Well, now that we've agreed we were both at fault…" I started to pivot.

"I'm glad you're here," he said. "Sit down and we can have the conversation I wanted to have last night."

Against my better judgment, I stayed put.

"You're from here originally and a federal agent," the chief said. "I thought you'd be a good resource for this case. I'm brand new, stepping into some pretty big shoes, from what I hear. She might open up more if she sees a friendly face."

"She who?"

"The chief's ex-wife, Margaret."

"What about Sean...Deputy Guthrie? He worked with the chief for years. He knows Margaret even better than I do."

"I'm getting information from him, too, but you're the one I'd like to pump..." He averted his gaze. "To get an insider's view."

Well, at least I wasn't alone in the fool-making category. "You've got a thing against gingers?" I asked. "Not that there's anything wrong with that. They are soulless spawns of Satan, after all."

Chief Fox chuckled. "Is that so? I'll have to be on my guard around him then. Now, if I can just ask you..." He shuffled papers around the desk, looking a little lost. I understood the feeling well, having been plonked down at Pidcock's messy desk recently.

"About the chief's ex-wife," I reminded him.

He stopped searching the papers and looked at me with relief in those sea-green eyes. "Yes, Margaret."

"They divorced years ago," I said. "There's no animosity between them." Unlike my parents. At least Chief O'Neill and Margaret were human and couldn't curse each other. Supernaturals had the ability to take toxic relationships to another level.

"Did you know that she's still listed as the beneficiary on his life insurance policy?"

That I did not know. "Is she aware of that?"

"If not, she'll know soon enough," Chief Fox said. "I'd like to get a sense of her knowledge before the lawyer gets to her."

"Smart. Who is the chief's lawyer?"

"Jayson Swift."

Ugh. I was surprised the chief would've chosen a shark like Jayson to handle his affairs.

"I can tell by your expression that you're not overly fond of the lawyer in question." A grin tugged at his lips.

"He's not one I would choose to represent my interests."

"I think your interests are well represented."

I arched an eyebrow. "What makes you say that?"

"I met some of your family last night," he said. "Your aunt's sweet, by the way."

"Great-aunt," I said. "Aunt Thora is my grandmother's sister."

"Right. She's the one who answered the door last night when I brought you home."

I closed my eyes, mortified that I'd forgotten to mention it, probably because I was keen to forget the whole thing. "Thanks for that. You didn't have to be the designated driver for me."

"It was a fun introduction to the residential section of town," he said. "You gave me a running commentary on your neighbors the whole way there."

My mouth suddenly became dry. "Did I?"

"Apparently, Mrs. Paulson is nosy and I should disregard everything she says. She likes to rant about fornication probably because she's never experienced it." He winked. "That's a direct quote."

I wanted to melt into the chair. "I'm sure she's not an eighty-year-old virgin." Almost sure.

"You also felt the need to mention that she was human." He laughed.

"Ha. Funny," I said wanly.

"So if you're free, why don't we head over to see Margaret O'Neill and you can give me running commentary on everyone we pass on the way?"

"How about I just sit quietly and not make a fool of myself?"

He flashed that megawatt grin. "That works too."

CHAPTER SEVEN

WE FOUND Margaret O'Neill on the tennis court at the Chipping Cheddar Country Club. She was mid-match against her instructor, the athletic and attractive Lance Hardaway. I wondered whether Margaret had any inkling that she was playing against a werewolf.

Lance sniffed the air as we approached. He cut me a curious glance when he saw me approach with Chief Fox.

"Is that you, Eden?" Margaret huffed as she whacked the ball across the court.

"Hi, Mrs. O'Neill," I said. "Good hit." I had no idea if that was the accepted expression. I knew next to nothing about tennis.

"It's Ms. Kowalski now," she said. "I finally went back to my maiden name a couple years ago. Seemed silly to keep the name when I didn't keep the man." She made eyes at Lance. She didn't seem to realize that Lance played for the other team—and I didn't just mean tennis.

"I'm sorry about the chief," I said. Divorced or not, I knew Margaret had to be struggling to come to terms with his sudden death.

"Thank you." She slammed the ball across the court with such force that Lance actually missed the return.

"I absolutely adore your intensity, Margaret," Lance said.

Margaret curtsied in response.

Chief Fox cleared his throat. I'd almost forgotten he was standing next to me.

"May I introduce the new chief?" I said. "Chief Fox, this is Margaret, Chief O'Neill's ex-wife."

Lance's gaze travelled over the chief. "Well, aren't you precious?" He tossed his racquet over his shoulder and crossed the court to shake the chief's hand. "Lance Hardaway. If you have any interest in joining the country club, I can definitely pull the necessary strings."

"It's not that kind of club," I said. "Anybody can join." As long as they could afford the fees.

"Nice to meet you both," Chief Fox said. "Ms. Kowalski, would you mind if I asked you a few questions about your husband? He left a lot of paperwork and I'm trying to make my way through it. It would be helpful to have your input."

"Of course, dear." She sashayed off the court, swinging her wide hips for Lance's benefit. Bless her.

Chief Fox glanced at Lance. "Would you mind giving us a few minutes? Maybe grab yourself a drink."

"How about I get you one while I'm at it, you thirsty boy?"

"I think you're the one who's thirsty, Lance," I said pointedly.

"I'll take a water," Chief Fox said. "Thanks." He seemed oblivious to Lance's efforts to charm him.

Lance headed back to the club with a spring in his step.

"What is it you need to know?" Margaret asked. She dropped onto the bench, letting her fatigue show now that Lance was gone.

"According to documents in my possession, you're still

the recipient of your ex-husband's insurance policy," the chief said.

I watched Margaret closely for a reaction.

"That doesn't surprise me in the least," she said. "He was never good about following through with things. Why do you think I'm the one who filed for divorce? If I didn't take care of something during our marriage, it didn't happen. Vacations? Bills to be paid? I did it all."

"He was dedicated to his job," I said, almost apologetically.

"That he was," Margaret agreed. "At the expense of his marriage. Nothing else mattered."

"To be fair, it is an all-encompassing job," Chief Fox said. "That's why I'm still single."

I'd kind of hoped he was single, so it was nice to have it confirmed. Not that I planned to date him. I only just moved back to town. The last thing I needed was to start a relationship with the new chief of police and set tongues wagging. As an FBM agent, I had an obligation to stay below the radar and do my job without attracting attention.

"So you didn't know about the insurance policy?" I asked.

She grunted. "Nope. How much is it?"

"Seven hundred and fifty thousand dollars," Chief Fox replied.

She whistled. "Are you serious?"

"I'm surprised you didn't know," I said. "If you were responsible for all the paperwork."

"The policy was acquired during the marriage," Chief Fox added.

Margaret stared into space. "I'd pestered him about getting one for ages. His line of work was dangerous, and I worried a lot when we were younger. I never wanted to be a young widow. I didn't realize he'd actually done it."

"Well, he did it," Chief Fox said. "Do you know his attorney, Jayson Swift?"

Margaret snorted. "Unfortunately. Is he the one I should talk to?"

"I'm sure he'll be getting in touch," Chief Fox said.

"Any idea why the chief was at the waterfront the day he died?" I asked. It was a long shot, but worth asking.

"I didn't keep up with Mick's schedule," Margaret said. "I did think it was odd when I heard how he died, though. Mick avoided water whenever possible. He wouldn't even honeymoon in Barbados like I wanted to. No islands, he said." She shook her head. "He was such a stubborn fool. I should've known right then the marriage wouldn't last."

Chief Fox's interest was piqued. "Why did he avoid water?"

"Because he couldn't swim," Margaret said. "Never learned and then was too old and embarrassed to get lessons. He didn't advertise the fact, but you'd never see him at the pool here at the club."

"Funny place to live for a man who hates water," Chief Fox said. "You've got the Chesapeake on one side and the river, too."

"He grew up here," Margaret said. "He wouldn't leave unless..." She sighed. "Well, only death could part him from Chipping Cheddar. The O'Neill family goes back generations in this town."

"Any reason to think someone would want to hurt him?" the chief asked.

Margaret met his penetrating gaze. "He was the chief of police. I'm sure there were plenty of people who wanted to hurt him."

Chief Fox didn't flinch. "What about his personal life? The family that's been here for generations? Any grudges you're aware of?"

Margaret appeared thoughtful. "He and his brother Ted had a longstanding dispute over the parcel near Cheddar Gorge."

"A parcel of land?" Chief Fox asked.

"A family property," Margaret said. "Their uncle had left it behind when he died but he didn't have a will. Ted insisted that he was the favorite nephew and their uncle would've left it solely to him."

"The uncle died without a wife or children of his own?" I asked.

"That's right," Margaret said. "Lots of girlfriends but never one good enough to marry in his eyes. Probably for the best. He was a philanderer anyway. He wouldn't have made any woman a good husband."

"Where can I find Ted O'Neill?" Chief Fox asked.

"The lighthouse," Margaret and I replied in unison.

The chief blinked. "He lives in the lighthouse?"

"No, he works there," I said.

"But he spends a lot of time there," Margaret added. "It's your best bet to catch up with him."

"Great, thanks for your help," the chief said. He retrieved a card from his pocket and handed it to Margaret. "If you think of anything else, will you let me know?"

She took the card. "You think I don't know the chief's number by heart?"

The chief gave her a sympathetic smile. "I'm sorry for your loss, Ms. Kowalski."

"Thank you."

Lance returned with two bottles of water and handed one to Chief Fox. "To quench your thirst, Chief."

"Thank you, Lance." The chief unscrewed the lid and took a deep drink, his lips wrapped around the bottle's neck.

I watched Lance's reaction with amusement. He gaped at the handsome chief with his mouth hanging open.

"Show's over, Lance," I whispered, as the chief put the lid back on the bottle.

Lance clamped his mouth closed.

"Shall we resume play?" Margaret asked her instructor.

"Yes, I believe I need to work off some energy," Lance replied.

"It was nice meeting you," Chief Fox said. "I'm sure I'll see you around. Thanks again for the water."

"Thanks again for the dreams I'll be having tonight," Lance said, softly enough that only I could hear him.

I suppressed a laugh.

Chief Fox and I walked back to the car in silence. Only when I slid into the passenger seat did he finally speak.

"What do your instincts tell you, Agent Fury?"

"She's innocent," I said.

"That's what I figured," the chief said. He put the car in reverse and pulled out of the parking spot. "Where can I drop you?"

"You don't want to talk to Ted?" I asked.

"I have a few inquiries to make before I'm ready to do that."

"Like get the deed information for the property?"

He cast me a sidelong glance. "Among other things."

"Ted is an interesting character," I said.

"I guess so if he spends most of his time in a lighthouse," he said.

"I don't mind coming with you when you go," I said, and then quickly added, "if you want someone to smooth the path for you."

"Ted's that much of a character, huh?"

I wore a vague smile. "You'll see."

. . .

I opened the door to my father's kitchen and was surprised to see my cousin Rafael and his family, as well as a man I didn't recognize.

Rafael broke into a broad smile when he saw me. "Will you look at that absolute vision of loveliness, everyone?" He stood at the counter with a variety of ingredients spread in front of him. As a warlock and a master chef with his own restaurant in town called Chophouse, Rafael was never far from a chopping board.

I crossed the kitchen to give Rafael a hard squeeze. "Hey, cousin."

"Eden, we're so happy you're home." His wife Julie planted a wet kiss on my cheek. Julie and their sixteen-year-old daughter, Meg, are werewolves. No one knew what to expect when Rafael and Julie got married. We'd never had a shifter in the family before, but, by all accounts, Rafael and Julie were blissfully happy.

"Our little flower girl is all grown up," Rafael said, smiling. He glanced at his wife. "Remember our wedding?"

"How can I forget? Not every flower girl eats the flower petals she's meant to be scattering," Julie said, and sighed at the happy memory. "You were so entertaining."

I held up a hand. "Okay, no reminders necessary."

Julie beamed. "I want to hear more about this. Did you get sick? Were they poisonous?"

"Speaking of trips down memory lane," my father interrupted, "Eden, do you remember Gustav, my old friend from university?"

I squinted at the squat man with the bushy white mustache. Although I remembered vague stories of pranks and shenanigans from their university days, I didn't recall much else about Gustav.

"Nice to see you, Gustav," I said politely.

"He's in town for a little while," my father said. "Isn't that great? It's just like old times."

Sally offered a pained smile. "Yes, they've already dusted off some of their old tomes."

I gave my dad a sharp look. "Do. Not. Summon. Anything." I already had Chief O'Neill's death to deal with. I didn't need to clean up my father's mess.

Gustav waved his hand. "Not to worry. There's no time for anything major. I'm on my way to visit my sister in Wilmington. I just couldn't pass up the opportunity to see my old roommate." He whacked my father on the back.

"Gustav brought news from Otherworld, too," Sally said. "He was kind enough to drop in on my Aunt Sara before coming here."

"She sent me with this." Gustav gestured to the miniature ceramic dragon on the counter. "It took ages to get through security and customs because of one tiny trinket."

"But I do appreciate it," Sally said. "Aunt Sara is so talented. I'm glad to see she's still creating."

"Her place was full of ceramic dragons," Gustav said. "I was tempted to get one for my nephew—he's obsessed with dragons—but I figured I'd wait until I go back."

"And what's your creation, Rafael?" I asked, inclining my head toward the counter.

"He's making a potion for your father's rheumatism," Sally said.

"Why can't you get one from Mom?" I asked. My mother's side was perfectly adept at making potions.

My father pulled a face. "I don't want to be poisoned. I want relief."

"Mom would never poison you," I said.

My father barked a short laugh. "You've clearly forgotten our trip to Cabo."

"That was the water!"

"That's what she wants you to think," my dad replied.

"I don't mind making it," Rafael said. "I figure it's a good teachable moment for Meg."

The teenager rolled her eyes. "I'm a werewolf. I don't do potions."

"You're a teenager," Julie said. "It seems to me you don't do much of anything."

"There's magic in your blood," Rafael said, pointing the knife at her while he spoke. "You can be like a wizard and learn spells from books."

Meg rested her chin in the palm of her hand. "Fine. Carry on."

Rafael inhaled deeply, preparing to work. He'd always had a flair for the dramatic. "One does not simply *cut* the eye of newt. One must *dice* it." He wiggled the knife. "But in order to properly bruise the lemongrass, I must use the dull side of the blade."

Meg pretended to snore. "You can imagine what he's like when he cooks dinner at home."

"So the cheese and crackers aren't part of the potion making?" I asked. The plate of nibbles nearby was making my mouth water.

"Help yourself," Sally said. "The cheese is local."

"I'd be disappointed if it wasn't," I replied. I took one cracker and plopped a chunk of cheese on top. Delicious. I often wondered whether I'd love cheese as much if I'd grown up elsewhere. The answer was probably.

"How's the investigation?" Sally asked, immediately wiping away the trail of crumbs I left on the counter. "Any leads?"

"None that have panned out so far," I said. "I'm meeting the new chief to interview a suspect." I didn't mention Ted's name. I knew they'd object to me even questioning Chief O'Neill's brother. For evil supernaturals, they were oddly loyal.

"I was sorry to hear about the chief," Rafael said. "He was a frequent customer in the restaurant. The man liked his porterhouse."

"Such a nice man," Julie agreed. "He caught me in the woods once—I'd forgotten to take my blocker that month and had shifted—and he didn't bat an eye. Thought I was naked because I was hooking up with a boy."

Meg's jaw unhinged. "What happened?"

"He got me a blanket from his patrol car to preserve my modesty," Julie said. "Told me to go home before I ran into any trouble." She smiled vacantly. "He didn't have a clue, bless him."

Meg popped a piece of cheese into her mouth. "I will *never* forget to take my blocker."

"I met this Chief Fox at the Cheese Wheel," my father said. "I don't care for him."

Rafael handed him the finished potion and my dad gulped it down without protest.

"He seems okay," I said. I didn't want to sound too defensive and risk an inquisition.

"If Mick's death isn't avenged…" my dad began.

I cut him off. "We don't even know if there's anything to avenge. It still might have been an accident." I didn't want my father getting any ideas. It was one thing to carry out revenge plans in other jurisdictions, but he had to realize what a difficult position he'd put me in to take action here.

"Eden's on the case, Uncle Stanley," Meg said. "She'll keep the new chief on his toes."

"Or on his back from what I've heard," Sally murmured.

I fixed her with a hard stare. "I need to go, but it was good to see everyone. Enjoy your visit, Gustav. Try to keep my dad out of trouble."

"We're going out tonight," Gustav said. "So no promises."

"Take more cheese," my dad said. He pushed the plate toward me. "You can't reap vengeance on an empty stomach."

"Dad!" My father was exasperating at times. "Vengeance is not my job. I'm an FBM agent."

"You're a fury, first and foremost." My father cracked his knuckles. "But if you can't handle it, let me know when you find the culprit and I'll be happy to administer my particular brand of vengeance."

"Stanley, mind your joints," Sally admonished him.

"I'll see you all later," I said. Now that my father was threatening to take action, I felt more motivated than ever to find out what happened to Chief O'Neill.

CHAPTER EIGHT

THE CHIPPING CHEDDAR lighthouse is one of the town's most iconic structures. It towered over the Chesapeake Bay, providing navigational assistance to the bevy of boats that frequented the area. Ted had served as the lighthouse keeper for as long as I could remember. Between the O'Neill brothers, the town was well protected.

"So what makes this guy such a character?" Chief Fox asked. He parked the police car not far from the lighthouse. I was trying to ignore the fact that he smelled like fresh pine and sea salt. If a candle existed with his scent, I'd totally buy it.

"He never married…" I began.

"Oh, well, now I understand."

I frowned. "You're teasing me."

"It's kind of fun," he replied. "An added benefit of our official time together."

There it was. Official. Although I knew he only desired my company in a professional capacity, I couldn't help but wish he had a personal ulterior motive.

"I guess I'll have to go back to my dark office when this is all over."

"Your office is dark?" he asked. "Do they have you in a dungeon or something?"

I explained my location between the donut shop and tattoo parlor.

"But donuts," the chief said encouragingly.

"True, but last time I checked, donuts don't provide natural light."

"They do have holes," he said.

I laughed. "I'll bear that in mind."

We vacated the car and trudged toward the lighthouse. The air wrapped around me like a warm blanket and I heard the call of seagulls overhead. I didn't blame Ted for spending so much time here. It was an idyllic spot.

"How many steps?" Chief Fox asked.

"Why? You don't look out of shape," I said.

He puffed out his chest. "We strippers need to keep our physiques up to snuff."

The back of my neck grew warm at the mention of my Cheese Wheel faux pas. "I'll go first. I haven't seen Ted since I've been back."

"That's the whole point of bringing you," the chief said. "Friendly face first."

"I'm not sure how I feel about being used like this." I started the long, winding climb to the top.

"Hey, I'm helping you with your Vitamin D intake. If you handle cyber crimes, you must sit in that dark office all day."

"I make an effort to stay active."

"I can see that." I couldn't be sure, because unlike my mother, I didn't have eyes in the back of my head, but I had the burning sensation that the chief was watching my backside all the way up the steps.

"Is that my kung pao chicken?" Ted called when we reached the top.

"Afraid not," I said, stepping into the circular space at the top of the lighthouse.

Ted's eyebrows knitted together. "Eden?" He wore goggles on top of his head, causing his white hair to stick up around them. He was dressed in a white karate outfit complete with an orange belt. He reminded me of Dr. Emmett Brown from *Back to the Future* in that weird and wonderful way.

"Hi, Ted," I said.

Ted's gaze flickered to the chief behind me. "And who's your friend?" He then seemed to notice Chief Fox's uniform and badge. "Oh. You're the new chief?"

"Nice to meet you, Ted. I'm Chief Sawyer Fox. I'm terribly sorry about your brother. I've heard a lot of great things about him since my arrival." He shook Ted's hand.

"Are you old enough to be a chief?" Ted asked. "You look like you're still in college."

"No, sir," Chief Fox replied. "Not for quite some time."

Ted nodded absently before shifting his focus back to me. "Are you home for a visit?"

"No, I moved back for work."

Ted chuckled. "I owe your Aunt Thora twenty bucks. She said you'd be back the day you left, but I thought for sure we'd seen the last of you."

"You remember a bet with my aunt?" I asked. "That would've been years ago."

Ted tapped the side of his head. "My bank account might be empty but my memory bank is full."

"Which kind of martial arts do you do?" the chief asked.

Ted stared at him. "I beg your pardon?"

Chief Fox gestured to his attire. "You're an orange belt. Is it Shotokan or something else?"

"I don't partake in any such activity," Ted replied.

The chief shot me a helpless look. I didn't know what to say. I warned him that Ted was a character. I decided to change the subject.

"This is the best view in town, Ted," I said. I walked to the window and surveyed the boats in the bay as the sunlight reflected off the water. A perfect day.

"It really is spectacular, isn't it?" Ted said. "I never tire of it." He joined me at the window. "You know your aunt and I spent many a romantic evening up here in our youth."

I held my hands over my ears. I didn't want to hear racy details about my sweet Aunt Thora. Ted didn't know about my family's heritage. According to family gossip, my great-aunt had broken up with Ted to save him from heartache. She knew she couldn't marry him, not without inflicting my family upon him and introducing him to a world he wasn't equipped to handle. She ended up marrying my Uncle Cyrus, an excessus demon, and they had my Uncle Moyer and Aunt Charisma. Uncle Cyrus died before I left Chipping Cheddar.

"Is Thora the sweet aunt that I met?" Chief Fox asked.

"Yes," I said, removing my hands. Only my great-aunt would find someone like Ted endearing. Of all my family members, she was the one I most identified with. Beneath her witchy exterior beat a soft heart. Even her choice of a demon husband had been relatively tame. As an excessus demon, Uncle Cyrus encouraged excessive behavior, especially in drinking, smoking, and gambling. He was the voice that whispered in their ears to keep going.

Ted tugged on his ear. "What brings you to the lighthouse? Is this a routine call for the new chief?"

"Not routine," the chief replied. "I'm investigating your brother's murder."

His eyes bulged. "Murder?" Ted repeated. "Someone murdered him? I thought he fell in the bay and drowned."

"Well, technically, he did," the chief said. "The question is who put him there?"

"Why do you think someone put him there?" Ted asked. "My brother couldn't swim. He could easily have fallen in and not been able to get out."

"According to others we've spoken to, your brother avoided the waterfront for that very reason," Chief Fox said. "Does it make sense to you that he was close enough to the bay to fall in?"

Ted shook his head and muttered, "No, I suppose it doesn't."

"What can you tell me about the property near Cheddar Gorge?" Chief Fox asked.

Ted squinted in confusion. "Uncle Gordon's land? What does that have to do with anything?"

"You tell me," the chief said. "It's come to my attention that you and your brother had a longstanding dispute over the parcel of land. Why don't you tell me more about it?"

Ted blew a raspberry. "No one can possibly think I'd kill my own brother over a patch of dirt and trees." He whipped off the goggles and placed them on a nearby mannequin.

I became fixated on the mannequin for a brief moment. How I missed it when I came in I had no idea.

"Um, Ted? What's with the mannequin?" There was a face drawn on the blank canvas and it wore a pink floral dress.

"That's Mildred," Ted replied.

Chief Fox maintained a neutral expression, but I knew he had to be wondering exactly how insane Ted was on a scale of one to Lizzie Borden.

"It gets lonely up here sometimes," Ted admitted. "Mildred is good company."

My chest tightened, realizing the extent of Ted's loneliness. "I talk to myself," I blurted. The people pleaser in me wanted to make Ted feel less awkward about his admission.

"You do?" Chief Fox turned toward me.

"Your Aunt Thora does that, too," Ted said. He smiled to himself, as though recalling a particular memory. "Mildred and I like to dance."

"Sounds nice," I said.

Chief Fox cleared his throat. "Can we get back to the property dispute?"

"I didn't see why Mick wanted it," Ted said. "He had his own piece of land with a nice house."

"Did he lose it in the divorce, though?" I asked.

Ted chewed his lip. "He did, but he rebounded quickly enough. Got another place. Still didn't build on the property."

"Probably because the two of you hadn't worked out an agreement," I pointed out.

"That land was meant for me," Ted said.

"You want to build a house on it?" Chief Fox asked.

"No, I don't want anyone to build on it," Ted said. "I want to keep it in its natural state. That's why I want to protect it from falling into the wrong hands."

"You think your brother's hands would have been the wrong ones?" I asked.

"No, but he was married to Margaret at the time," Ted said. "I worried what she would do with it."

"And what about after the divorce?" Chief Fox asked. "By all accounts, you were still fighting over it."

"Not really," Ted said. "We just hadn't talked about it in recent years. It had been such a sore subject." He shuddered. "I don't like family drama."

That made two of us.

"Well, you can breathe a sigh of relief because the property is legally yours now," Chief Fox said. "If you're concerned about its future, though, make sure you address it in your will."

"I've got it covered, Chief," Ted said. "Thanks, though."

We'd already lost one O'Neill this week. It wasn't worth contemplating Ted's demise as well.

"Is there anyone you can think of that would have wished your brother harm?" the chief asked.

"I suppose you haven't talked to Lawrence Whitaker."

"Who's that?" I asked. The name didn't ring a bell.

Chief Fox snapped his fingers. "He was a recent arrest. I saw his file on the chief's desk." He stroked his dimpled chin. "I didn't notice anything unusual about the case."

"That's because my brother didn't mention it to anyone except me," Ted said. "Mick knew Lawrence from golf. They were part of some group that met for games."

"And the chief had to arrest him?" I asked.

"The charges didn't stick, whatever they were," Ted said. "Can't remember, but Mick said that Lawrence threatened him."

Well, this was new information. "What was he arrested for, Chief?"

"I'll need to consult the file," Chief Fox said. "But thanks for the lead, Mr. O'Neill. It's very helpful."

Ted lowered his head. "I want to know what happened to my brother as much as you do. He was the only family I had left." He glanced at the mannequin. "It's just you and me now, Mildred."

"It was great to see you again, Ted."

The lighthouse keeper adjusted his orange belt. "You, too. Give my regards to Thora." He smiled at the mannequin. "We wouldn't mind a visit from Thora, would we, Mildred? She'd be a welcome addition to our dance card."

"I'll be in touch, Mr. O'Neill," the chief said, ushering me toward the exit.

I hurried down the winding staircase before there was any mention of a threesome.

. . .

According to the report, Lawrence Whitaker had been arrested for drunk driving. Chief O'Neill had made the arrest himself on a Sunday afternoon at four o'clock, not far from the country club. Lawrence hired none other than Jayson Swift to defend him, which explained why the charges didn't stick. One more reason to dislike the slimy lawyer.

"Does Deputy Guthrie know anything about this?" I asked. We were in the chief's office reviewing the file for helpful details.

"Let's find out," Chief Fox replied. He hit the buzzer on the landline. "Deputy, are you here?"

Sean appeared in the doorway two minutes later. He scowled when he noticed me in the chair. I was tempted to stick out my tongue but thought better of it.

"Do you know anything about the arrest of Lawrence Whitaker?" Chief Fox asked.

Sean pursed his lips. "I remember that the chief wasn't happy about arresting him, but he was even less happy when he got off."

"I understand the two men were friends," Chief Fox said. "Is that true?"

"I know they played golf together sometimes," Sean said. "But as part of a bigger group."

"Whitaker's address is on Abertam Road," Chief Fox said, reading from the report. "Where's that?"

"I don't know it," I said.

"Newer construction," Sean said. "McMansion types."

Oh. Why didn't that surprise me?

Chief Fox looked at me. "How about it, Agent Fury? Sick of me yet?"

"I'm not, Chief," Sean said quickly.

"I need you on patrol," Chief Fox said. "To be honest, I was surprised to find you here now."

"This isn't Des Moines," Sean said. "Chipping Cheddar is a small town."

"A small town with murders and drunk drivers, apparently," Chief Fox replied. "Best get out there, Deputy."

"Yes, sir," he said, and glowered at me for good measure before disappearing.

"I guess both of us are flying blind here," Chief Fox said.

"Abertam Road didn't exist when I lived here before," I said. "The development is probably on the land that was the old Coverdale farm." The Wentworths and the Coverdales had once owned two of the largest dairy farms in town. My family now owned the Wentworths' land, but the Coverdale land had been tied up in litigation for years when I was a kid. Not anymore, I guess.

We drove to the outskirts of town and I was amazed to see the size of the houses on what was once acres of farmland.

Lawrence Whitaker's house was the grandest of them all. It was situated at the end of the road, set back so far that we had to drive down a tree-lined lane to reach the semi-circular driveway. I knew there were wealthy people in Chipping Cheddar, but I didn't often rub elbows with them. My family had always been suspicious of people with 'too much' money. I wasn't sure what qualified as 'too much' in their view, but I suspected that Lawrence Whitaker fit the bill.

"Nice little shack," Chief Fox remarked. He parked the car right in middle of the semi-circular driveway.

"Do you think he has a butler?"

"We'll find out when we ring the bell."

Lawrence did not have a butler. He did, however, have a wife and two teenaged children. Their portraits were framed all over the walls of the entryway. His wife answered the door and let us in with a puzzled look.

"Is Kenny in trouble?" Mrs. Whitaker asked. She was a statuesque woman with auburn hair and a few fine lines around her mouth. Her forehead, on the other hand, suggested monthly Botox injections. "I warned him to slow down on school roads." She gave an apologetic smile. "New drivers, you know how they are."

"I'm not here about your son, Mrs. Whitaker," the chief said. "We'd like to speak with your husband."

Her eyes widened slightly. "Lawrence is in his office. Right this way, please."

I tried not to gape at the furnishings as we passed through the house. Every piece of furniture appeared to be worth a small fortune. Georgian highboys and Queen Anne accent chairs. No Pottery Barn for the Whitakers.

"Lawrence, Chief..." Mrs. Whitaker squinted at his badge. "Chief Fox is here to see you with his lovely assistant."

"I'm not his assistant," I said.

"This is Agent Fury," Chief Fox said. "FBI."

Lawrence and his wife both appeared stunned.

"Can I offer you anything to drink?" she asked, quickly recovering.

"No, thank you," I said.

"Mr. Whitaker, if you don't mind, we'd like to ask you a few questions," the chief said.

Lawrence Whitaker was a slightly balding man in a crisp blue collared shirt. He sat behind a substantial mahogany desk.

"What is this regarding?" Lawrence asked.

"Chief O'Neill," I said.

Lawrence flinched. "Sad news about the chief. We played golf together."

"We understand he also arrested you last month," Chief Fox said.

Lawrence reached for the cell phone on his desk. "I think I'll call my lawyer."

"No need for a lawyer," the chief said. "We're just talking."

Lawrence's nostrils flared. "I don't have anything to say."

"Because you pushed Chief O'Neill into the bay?" Chief Fox asked. "I can understand why you wouldn't want to admit that."

Lawrence released his grip on the phone. "I wasn't even in town the day Mick died."

Well, there went that theory.

"Where were you?" I asked.

"I was in Miami on a business trip. I came home the following evening. You can check my records." He tapped the screen of his phone. "In fact, I still have my ticket in my Apple wallet." He showed us the screen.

"We'll still need to confirm that you actually boarded the flight," the chief said.

"Do whatever you need to do," Lawrence said snidely. "But if you need anything else from me, you'll have to call Jayson Swift."

"Thank you for your time." Chief Fox pushed back the chair and stood. "You should know that if I ever catch you drinking and driving in this town, there isn't a fancy lawyer on earth that will be able to extricate you from those charges."

Lawrence tipped an imaginary cap. "I consider myself warned."

Now he was the kind of guy I wouldn't necessarily mind handing over to my family for their special brand of justice.

We left the office and found Mrs. Whitaker hovering by the front door. "I'm sorry about that," she said. "He's generally better behaved."

"He's a grown man, not a toddler," I replied. "And his type of bad behavior can have serious consequences."

She wrung her hands. "He's promised me he'll get help." She kept her voice low so as not to be overheard.

Chief Fox gave her a stern look. "For your sake, I hope he does. If he doesn't, he'll be trading the bar for a whole set of them."

CHAPTER NINE

I AWOKE the next morning to find the house buzzing with the arrival of more relatives—apparently, Uncle Moyer and his husband, Tomas, had been invited to breakfast to celebrate my return home, not that anyone bothered to tell me.

I climbed down the steps, still dressed in my favorite heart pajamas.

"Eden, you spectacular creature. Come here." Tomas opened his arms wide and I wrapped mine around his taut waist.

"Still working out, huh?" I asked. Solid abs didn't lie.

"Gotta look good to do good," Tomas replied.

"You really don't," I said, releasing him. "But that's okay."

"There's nothing wrong with a little vanity," my mother said. She gave Tomas a kiss on the cheek. "In fact, some of us could use a little more of it. Might help with her dating life, or lack thereof." She fluttered her eyelids in my direction.

"What about your uncle? My abs aren't solid enough for you?" Uncle Moyer gave me his version of an embrace, which involved a one-armed hug and two firm pats on the back as though he were burping me.

"It's great to see you both," I said. "Tomas, your hair is lighter again." They'd stopped in to visit me in San Francisco two years ago during their tour of wine country.

Tomas ran a hand through his golden hair. "The sun works wonders, my dear."

"Not for Eden's hair," Grandma interjected. "It absorbs all the light. It's like a black hole."

Tomas's gaze flicked from me to my mother. "Seeing you two together again—Beatrice, you could be Eden's older sister."

I tensed. "You realize that's a compliment for her and not for me, right?"

My mother fingered her gold necklace. "And what? I don't deserve compliments anymore? I've aged out?"

"When do I age in?" I queried.

"Would anyone like a slice of fresh lemon in their tea?" Aunt Thora asked.

Uncle Moyer and Tomas raised their hands.

"The smell of lemons is just heavenly," my great-aunt said, inhaling the scent before placing the lemon on the chopping board.

"Like you would know," Grandma said. "The nearest you've been to Heaven is Tomas over here."

"Same," Uncle Moyer said with a devilish grin.

My mother handed me a cup of tea and I sat at the round table with our visitors.

"How's your practice?" I asked Uncle Moyer.

Tomas rubbed his husband's back. "Voted best in the county three years straight now."

"They don't call him Moyer the Lawyer for nothing," Aunt Thora said. She placed a cup of tea in front of each man.

"They call him that because he *is* a lawyer," Grandma said.

"And it rhymes," Uncle Moyer said. "Tomas the Lawyer doesn't have the same ring to it."

Tomas winked. "And I'm far too lazy to practice law. I leave the hard work to my gorgeous husband. True grit makes him even more attractive, if that's possible."

"I guess the state bar doesn't know about your extracurricular law practice," I said.

"Certainly not," Uncle Moyer replied. "They would disbar me on the grounds of insanity if I told them I was actually a demon drafting contracts with humans."

"To trade their souls," Grandma said proudly. "It's like I raised you myself."

"My practice isn't as niche as that," Uncle Moyer said.

"According to the information I've been reading, the FBM has had to intervene in many cases involving demon lawyers," I said.

Uncle Moyer sipped his tea. "I don't doubt it. There are far too many unscrupulous lawyers out there willing to dupe unsuspecting humans into unfair bargains."

I blew steam off the surface of my tea. "You don't think it's unfair to take the souls of humans?"

Uncle Moyer straightened in his seat. "My contracts are always clear and in the common tongue," he said. "I don't want any disgruntled parties. It only results in headaches down the road for me."

My mother sailed over to the table with a plate of croissants and set it in the middle. "You two are definitely a case of opposites attract if ever there was one," she said, and squeezed Tomas on the shoulders with both hands. "At this rate I'd be happy to attract anyone at all—opposite, similar, doesn't matter."

"You took the 'doesn't matter' approach the first time and look what happened," Grandma said.

"That's my father you're talking about," I said. I didn't

care that my mouth was stuffed full of buttery goodness.

"Are you sure?" Grandma said. "I didn't say the first time she got married."

I bit my tongue. This conversation could easily go downhill quickly if I let it.

"It isn't all smooth sailing with Tomas and I," Uncle Moyer admitted. "Sometimes the opposite issue can cause ripples on otherwise calm waters."

"Like when?" my mother asked. "You two have one of the best relationships in town."

Uncle Moyer and Tomas smiled at each other. One was as handsome as the other, especially when they were showing teeth.

"You know Tomas is supposed to act as an invisible hand in this world," Uncle Moyer said.

"I do dole out the goodness," Tomas said.

"Except he leaves his feathers everywhere," Uncle Moyer explained. "It's almost as though he wants credit for his good deeds."

"I'm only part angel," Tomas said, by way of explanation. "What can I say? The human part of me is sloppy."

"You should see his halo," Uncle Moyer continued. "I polish it every Wednesday because Tomas leaves his grubby fingerprints all over it."

"It's my halo," Tomas replied. "Who else's fingerprints should be on it?"

Uncle Moyer shook his head. "I'm just glad we have the time and money to combat these issues. I can't imagine couples with lots of kids and little money to outsource their burdens. No wonder the divorce rate is so high."

"You two are lucky in many ways," my mother said.

"And how about you, Miss Eden?" Tomas asked. "Have you been getting lucky in many ways?"

"Eden couldn't get lucky wearing a rabbit's foot tied to a horseshoe," Grandma said.

Tomas wrinkled his nose. "Certainly not. That outfit would put anyone off."

"I'm too busy to worry about dating," I said.

"You don't look busy," Uncle Moyer said, noting my heart pajamas and unkempt hair.

"She's here all the time, hiding in the attic and talking to herself," Grandma interjected. "She's like a hermit."

"I am not! I'm constantly out and about. That's what happens when you have a job."

Grandma gave me a sharp look. "Is that a dig at me? Let me tell you something, young lady. I've had plenty of jobs and raising your mother was the hardest one of them."

My mother's head jerked toward her. "Hey!"

"Well, maybe you'll meet someone in connection with your new job," Uncle Moyer said. "That's how I met Tomas, after all."

"Don't boink someone you get out of prison," Grandma said. "That might fly in Thora's branch of the family, but not mine."

"Firstly, no one says boink," Uncle Moyer replied. "Secondly, Tomas was imprisoned for protesting. He's a social justice warrior."

Tomas shrugged. "I am that."

"Just out of curiosity, what does the FBM have you doing?" Uncle Moyer asked. "Are you acting as a guardian in case the portal reopens?"

I shuddered at the prospect of the portal ever reopening. "No, it's more straightforward. Any use of magic in my jurisdiction gets investigated."

"Not *any* use," my mother interjected. "You don't go after us for making potions to heal."

"Or hinder," Aunt Thora added, with an accusatory look at my grandmother.

"No, we don't tend to bother with small traces of magic like that," I said. "Or good magic."

"Why not good magic?" Tomas asked. "It seems to me that can be as disruptive to human life as bad magic."

"Because we generally see so little of it," I said. "There was an executive order a few decades ago to cease all interference with good magic."

"So the tooth fairy continues her dark reign," Uncle Moyer said, his jaw tightening.

"You have issues with the tooth fairy?" I asked.

He frowned at me. "She collects the bones of children and pays good coin for them. She may as well be harvesting their organs."

"Well, when you put it that way..." I wasn't about to argue with Uncle Moyer. He could browbeat anybody under the table with logic, except maybe Grandma.

A knock on the door interrupted our discussion. "I'll get it," my mother said and disappeared around the corner. She returned a moment later with Clara behind her. Everyone made a fuss over my old friend, making her feel welcome, and I felt a rush of warmth for my family. They had their shining moments—few and far between—but they had them nonetheless.

"I am so thrilled to see the two of you making trouble again," my mother said, giving Clara a squeeze.

"Yeah, about time you ditched that walking set of boobs," Grandma said to Clara. "I've seen the two of you in town and it made my skin crawl every time."

"That's the lotion I made for you," Aunt Thora said. "I told you it was made with crushed cockroaches."

Clara took the dig at Sassy in stride. "I'm definitely glad

to have Eden back. There are some holes that can only be filled by a particular person."

I smiled up at her. "You just want the rest of my croissant, don't you?"

"Are you offering?"

I passed her the half a croissant. "Why don't I show you my fancy digs? I need to get dressed anyway."

"She means the attic," Grandma said.

"Thanks for the interpretation." I scraped back my chair. "It was so great to see you. Thanks for coming over."

"We expect to see a lot more of you now that you're home for good," Uncle Moyer said.

For good.

I resisted the shiver that threatened to overtake me. Instead, I grabbed Clara by the hand and we headed up to the attic to talk in private.

"You're really living in the attic?" Clara surveyed the boxes and cobwebs. "No one even bothered to clean?"

"It's only temporary," I said. "I'm sorry about what Grandma said about Sassy. That was rude."

"But not surprising." Clara sat on the mattress while I got dressed. "Sassy is misunderstood. Once you get to know her, you'll understand her behavior better. She's more vulnerable than we ever realized."

"Well, sure. If I puncture her artery, she's vulnerable," I said. Wishful thinking, I knew.

Clara wore a vague smile. "Your brand of violence has always been more verbal than physical."

"And I'm so sorry about the way I treated you," I blurted. "I know I wasn't a good friend and I want you to know that I do feel terrible about it. I have for years."

Clara took my hand and I felt a jolt. Grief washed over me and I instantly knew what I was experiencing. Clara's feelings. She was experiencing my emotions as an empath, while my magic siphoning skills were allowing me to experience hers. We both began to cry.

"Oh, Eden. I'm so glad you're home." Clara released my hand in order to throw her arms around me and the connection broke.

"I promise to never do anything like that again," I said. I'd bottled up my feelings for so long, and now the emotional dam was bursting.

"I sort of understood," Clara said. "Even without you telling me. You were never happy here." She pulled back and inclined her head to study me. "But now you're back. I'm not really sure what to think."

I told her about what happened in San Francisco and how I ended up here.

"I'm so sorry, Eden," Clara said. "I know how much you wanted to have a normal human life."

I managed a smile. "It's okay. I'm glad to see you again and life at home isn't so bad."

Clara cocked an eyebrow. "I just felt your emotions, Eden. There's no need to lie."

I laughed. "Okay. Let's just say my feelings are complicated."

"I see Anton around sometimes," Clara said. "Your niece and nephew are adorable."

"Thanks. I'm just getting to know them. I'm not used to little ones."

"Think of it this way. You can be the guiding light that keeps them from succumbing to the dark side."

"I like that." I sat down to put on my socks and shoes. "Olivia is the one to watch. She's going to have powers. Ryan is less clear. They keep trying to coax the evil out of him, but I can't tell if it's futile. He's only a year old."

"There's plenty of time." She paused. "Not to change the

subject to a less pleasant topic, but have you had any luck with the investigation?"

"Nothing so far," I said. "Everyone's been cleared."

"That's too bad. How's Sean taking your involvement?" Clara stifled a giggle. "I can't imagine very well."

"I suspect he's taking the arrival of the new chief even less well," I said. "As much as I don't want to be evil, the whole thing fills me with joy."

"People can't stop talking about the new chief," Clara said.

"What have you heard?" I asked.

Clara smiled. "That he's much too handsome to be a cop in a backwater town like Chipping Cheddar. That's what Sassy's been telling everyone since that night at the Cheese Wheel."

Uh oh. "And has she already sent Tanner packing?"

Clara shook her head. "Have you seen him?"

"Briefly," I said. "I didn't linger."

"Probably for the best," Clara said. "He hasn't changed much. You noticed Sassy isn't wearing a ring. That's because Tanner keeps jerking her around. I know he's cheated on her, but Sassy refuses to believe it."

For a fleeting moment, I actually felt sorry for Sassy. "It's not like she can't meet someone else. Sassy is awful, but she's pretty."

Clara laughed. "That's what we used to call her, remember? Pretty awful?"

"But you two are friends now, so I guess that's not a good nickname."

Clara cast a sidelong glance at me. "It might surprise you to learn that Sassy has a decent sense of humor, even when it comes to herself. I've told her some of our stories from high school, even the ones that don't paint her in a good light, and she's been a great sport."

"You're right. It does surprise me." That didn't sound like the Sassy Persimmons I knew and loathed.

"I think the three of us should get together," Clara said. "Maybe if we spend time together, you'll come to see her as I do."

"We already did, at the Cheese Wheel." The evening went well. Why ruin it with another one?

"Here's the thing, Eden. Sassy and I are really close now. I'm thrilled that you're home and I want us to be close again. I've really missed you, but I'm not going to leave Sassy out. It isn't fair."

Clara was the most loyal person I knew. It was one of her best qualities, even if—right now—it was working against me.

"You're absolutely right," I said. "It would be unreasonable of me to expect you to drop Sassy. She's been a better friend to you than I have these past few years." As much as it pained me to say it, it was the truth.

"I forgive you." Clara and I stood at the same time and I nearly bumped my head on the slope of the attic ceiling. "I always knew you'd come back. This place wasn't the same without you."

My chest ached in response to her earnest admission. Leave it to an empath to activate my waterworks. "Thanks, Clara. That means more to me than you know."

My ringtone blasted, ruining the moment. The James Bond theme song filled the attic.

Neville.

"Excuse me," I said to Clara. "Duty calls." I tapped the screen. "What's up, Neville?"

"Sorry to bother you out of the office," he said. "I thought you'd want to know there's been another death in town."

"Another death?" I repeated. "A murder?"

"Not sure," Neville replied. "Someone just called the police station to report it."

"How do you know that?"

"I have listening devices planted all over town," Neville said. "Standard operating procedure."

Right. Why wouldn't the FBM eavesdrop on human law enforcement? I was totally comfortable with that—not.

"You'll want to hurry," Neville said. "It's Dr. Myslinski's office on Feta Street."

"The dentist?" I asked. That reminded me that I hadn't chosen a new dentist since my return home. I was fanatical about a cleaning every six months. Maybe I'd kill two birds... I cringed. I needed a better metaphor right now.

"Yes. He's at number twenty on the third floor," Neville said. "Chief Fox is headed over to the scene now."

I inhaled sharply. "Then so am I."

CHAPTER TEN

BY THE TIME I ARRIVED, Chief Fox and Deputy Guthrie were deep in conversation as the body was transported out of the building.

"What happened?" I interrupted. No point in waiting for them to notice me.

Chief Fox looked at me with surprise. "Agent Fury, how did you…?"

"I have a dentist appointment," I lied. I couldn't throw Neville under the bus. His listening devices were worth their weight in gold.

"So did Elliott Bradford," Sean said. "He never made it."

"He was found in the elevator," Chief Fox said. "Looks like a heart attack."

"Did the elevator malfunction?" I asked.

"We've asked the building manager to check. No one noticed an issue with the elevator until another patient tried to leave Dr. Myslinski's office. They hit the button multiple times until the doors finally opened."

"And she found Elliott dead on the elevator floor," Sean said.

"Do we think this is connected to Chief O'Neill?" I asked.

"I don't see how," Chief Fox replied. "Bradford was a sixty-five year old man. A heart attack isn't suspicious."

I was inclined to agree.

"Not every death is a murder, Eden," Sean said. "This isn't San Francisco."

"No, if this were San Francisco, you'd be asking if they want fries with that," I snapped.

Sean scratched his head. "Fries with what?"

"I'm about to call his wife," Chief Fox said. "Man, I hate this part of the job."

I empathized with that. "By the way, what happened with Lawrence Whitaker?"

"His alibi checked out," the chief said.

Disappointment settled in the pit of my stomach. I would have been perfectly happy to see a guy like Lawrence get his just desserts.

The entrance door flew open and a woman rushed into the lobby. Her hair was in curlers and she wore sweatpants paired with a pajama top. "Where is he? Where's my Elliott?"

Chief Fox moved to intercept her. "Are you Marianne Bradford?"

"Yes." She nodded vigorously.

"I'm Chief Fox. I'm afraid I have bad news about your husband."

Marianne's expression crumpled. "No, don't say it. If you don't say it, then it isn't real."

Chief Fox placed a comforting arm around her shoulders. "Mrs. Bradford, I'm sorry to tell you that your husband is dead."

Marianne began to whimper. "How? Was he mugged?"

"No, he wasn't mugged," the chief said.

"Are you sure? Because crime in this town has had an uptick since Chief O'Neill died," she said.

"It's been like a week," I said.

"Where did you hear that?" Sean asked. He seemed miffed, not that I blamed him.

Marianne flicked a dismissive finger. "Everyone's talking about it. I was in the salon yesterday and half the customers were putting Xanax in their protein shakes. That's how worried they are about their safety."

Chief Fox patted her arm. "The situation isn't dire, Mrs. Bradford. In fact, muggings in Chipping Cheddar are extremely rare."

"Then what happened to my husband?" she asked, blinking back tears.

"Heart attack," Sean said. "He was found in the elevator. We're not sure whether the elevator was stuck and he panicked or what. We're getting whatever information we can."

Marianne adjusted a loose curler in her hair. "What do you mean he was found in the elevator?"

Chief Fox pointed to the elevator. "It's right there. Dr. Myslinski's office is on the third floor."

Marianne glared at the offending machine. "*Now* he takes an elevator? I had to walk up twenty flights to our hotel on our honeymoon because Elliott hated elevators so much. Now he takes one? For three flights?" She blew a raspberry. "Ridiculous man."

"Elliott hated elevators?" I asked. "Why?"

"Why does anyone?" she replied. "He hated being confined in small spaces." She paused, dropping her gaze to the floor. "Oh, my. I just used the past tense to talk about my husband."

"Is there a problem with the stairs?" I asked.

Chief Fox and Sean exchanged glances. "We took the stairs when we got here," the chief said. "No problems there."

"Maybe he thought it was okay because it's only three flights?" Sean proposed.

"Then why not just take the stairs?" I asked. "Was he suffering from any injuries? A sore leg? A stubbed toe? Anything that would force him into the elevator?"

Marianne shook her head. "No, he was in pretty good shape for his age. One of the things I appreciated about him. Didn't let himself go." She touched her curlers. "I try not to, either."

"When you're ready, we need you to come down to the station and positively identify him," Chief Fox said.

Marianne gave him a blank look. "Identify my husband's body?"

"Yes," the chief said softly.

"Okay." She frowned. "Will you drive me? I always wanted to ride in the front of a police car."

Sean held up a finger. "But I ride…"

Chief Fox cut him off. "Yes, that's no trouble, Mrs. Bradford. Deputy Guthrie will ride in the back."

I suppressed a smile. "Mind if I come down to the station?" I didn't want to miss anything.

"I thought you had a dentist appointment," Sean said with a sneer.

"This is more important."

Chief Fox gave me a curious look. "I don't think you're needed on this one, Agent Fury, but thanks."

Of course he didn't think so. Why would the feds be interested in a man's elevator-induced heart attack? I still wasn't sure that I *was* interested, but Mrs. Bradford's reaction gave me pause. If he felt as strongly as his wife suggested, then why did Elliott choose to take the elevator?

· · ·

With no more leads in the investigation, I decided to stop by my dad's house and see if we could brainstorm for ideas. I opened the kitchen door and called his name.

"They're out to eat," a voice said.

I whirled around. "Gustav?" My heart was pounding. I'd completely forgotten about their visitor.

"Sorry, I didn't mean to startle you."

"No, it's okay. I didn't think anyone was here."

"I'm not here for long," he replied. "I'm supposed to meet them at a place called Fondue Paradise. Do you know it?"

"Oh, yes." My mouth watered at the mention of fondue. Melted cheese was one of my weaknesses. "You'll love it. It's downtown on one of the cute cobblestone side streets. Stilton Lane."

"Thanks. They're the best hosts a demon could ask for."

"I'll just leave him a note to say I was here." No point wasting Brownie points.

"I can tell him you stopped by," Gustav offered.

"That's okay. He'll appreciate it more if I write him a note." He'd consider a message via Gustav to be lazy.

"Suit yourself." I heard the front door open and close.

I was just finishing the note to my dad when a familiar figure materialized in front of me.

"Chief O'Neill? Is that you?" In my dad's kitchen?

"Eden? You can see me?" He looked around awkwardly. "I tried to talk to a handful of people, but no one answered."

"That's because you're dead," I said bluntly.

"I got that far," he said. "Why are you not panicking?"

"Because I've been able to see ghosts my entire life. It's one of my things."

His eyes slanted. "Can your whole family see ghosts?"

"Nope, that wonderful talent was relegated to yours truly."

"So no point in coming to talk to your dad then, huh?"

"No, but that's okay. You got me instead."

"Feels weird to be a ghost. I feel lighter." He whooshed around the room. "I even went to the golf course. That was interesting. Did you know Gary Jenkins cheats? I couldn't believe it."

"Do you happen to remember anything about your accident?" I asked.

"You mean drowning? That was pretty unpleasant business, let me tell you."

"Did you see anyone?"

Chief O'Neill stroked his transparent chin thoughtfully. "No, I just remember this overwhelming compulsion to look at the water." He swallowed hard. "I don't know why. I generally avoid it."

"Because you can't swim."

He glanced at me in surprise. "You knew?"

"Everyone knows."

"Right. I tried not to make a big deal about it. Guess I failed." He chuckled softly. "I always send Sean to investigate any incidents near the waterfront. I've had a fear of falling in and drowning for as long as I can remember." His smile faded. "I guess now I know why. Maybe I was a little bit psychic, like your friend Clara."

"Clara isn't psychic," I corrected him. "She's an empath. She feels the emotions of others. It's complicated."

"Oh." He drifted around the room, despondent. "I'm not sure how I feel about this whole dead thing."

"Sadly, it doesn't matter how you feel," I said. "You don't exactly get a choice in the matter."

"Tell your dad I didn't give him back all his golf clubs," he said sheepishly. "I kept the nine iron. It's in my garage, near the toolbox."

"I'll tell him."

Chief O'Neill floated around in a circle, getting accustomed to his new form. "Does your family know you can do this?"

"They do," I replied.

"Is that why you became a federal agent? Because you could ask the victims questions that no one else could?"

"No," I said. "I didn't use my ability as an FBI agent."

"You're using it now."

I released a breath. "I'm not just an FBI agent here, Chief. I work for the FBM."

His brow furrowed. "What's that?"

"Federal Bureau of Magic."

"There's no such thing," he scoffed.

It wasn't my job to convince him, so I let it go.

"Why am I still here?" he asked. "Why haven't I gone to Heaven?"

"Unfinished business usually," I said. "In your case, I'd say it's figuring out who murdered you."

Chief O'Neill stopped short. "Murdered me? Are you sure?"

"That's the consensus, and seeing your ghost now confirms it for me."

"Who would murder me?"

"That's the hot question." I paused. "Tell me everything you can remember about the day you died. Were you alone at the marina?"

"No, I passed a few people. Llewellyn James, Carolyn Hartness, Joe Lowe." He reeled off a few more names I recognized. "Last person I remember seeing is Wade Cantrell."

"Who's that?"

"He owns that big monster yacht that takes up half the bay," he said, clearly annoyed. "Hard to miss."

"Did you speak to Wade?"

"Yeah, I did. I gave him a citation. He wasn't happy about it. He's the kind of guy used to getting his own way."

"What was the citation for?"

"Reckless driving," he said. "The boat. A few complaints came in and I couldn't ignore them this time."

"You'd ignored previous complaints?"

The chief didn't look proud of himself. "You know how it is here, Eden. It's a sleepy town. We're not as by-the-book as other towns because we don't need to be. Heck, your own family would've been up a creek ten times over if I wasn't willing to overlook infractions on occasion."

That much was true. My family didn't flaunt their powers in town, but they definitely got themselves into a bind now and again. When Anton was a teenager, he went through a moody, back-talking stage until my mother used magic to hang him from the flagpole down-town by his underpants. Chief O'Neill had to use a fire truck ladder to get him down. Anton fell in line after that.

"Did Wade pay you not to cite him the previous times?" I asked, incredulous.

"No, no, it wasn't like that. I would never accept a bribe." He puffed out his chest. "I'm an honorable man."

"I know you are, Chief." I felt guilty for suggesting other-wise. "Why did you go yourself? Why not send Deputy Guthrie to give the citation?"

"Because it was Wade," the chief replied. "He's difficult. A little slippery, if you know what I mean. I didn't think Sean was up to the task. He can be a little…" He faltered.

"A little incompetent?" I offered. "A complete ass? It's okay, Chief. You're dead now. You can say these things and it won't get back to him."

Chief O'Neill dragged a hand through his hair, not seeming to realize he'd only slice the air. "He's not the worst deputy I've had."

"That's high praise, indeed." I laughed. "He's annoyed that

a new chief was brought in from out of town instead of promoting from within."

"Guthrie wasn't up for the job. He's an okay kid, but he doesn't have the chops."

"I think it's apparent to anyone who meets him that Sean isn't up for the challenge. Even the cashier in the grocery store could tell you as much." I thought about Wade Cantrell. "Do you think the citation was a strong enough motive?"

The chief glanced at me. "Motive for what?"

"To join the Daughters of the American Revolution," I cracked. I gestured to his ghostly appearance. "What do you think?"

Chief O'Neill chuckled. "You always were a smart ass like your father." His smile faded. "I honestly don't know. A guy like that...He definitely thinks he's above the law."

"Then we'll talk to him."

"We? So the new chief is investigating my death? What's he like?"

I nearly tripped over my tongue to avoid saying "hot." I made a noise at the back of my throat. "He seems to have his act together."

"Well, what's his story?" the chief pressed. "I assume he's younger than me."

"Oh, yes. No older than thirty, I'd say."

The chief whistled, which surprised me. I'd never heard a ghost whistle. "That is young. Younger than I was when I became chief." He eyed me closely. "He doesn't know the truth about you, does he?"

"You've known me my whole life and no one told you," I replied. "Do you really think I'd tell the hottest guy in town that I'm a demon spawn?" Oops.

The chief cut me a sharp glance. "Hottest guy in town, huh?" He wagged a finger at me. "Careful, Eden."

"There's nothing to be careful about. We're working

together. That's it." I steered the conversation back to his death. "You don't remember anyone pushing you? No hands on your back?" Even if he didn't see the culprit, he might remember the sensation of being shoved.

"No, nothing like that."

I was starting to wonder whether this wasn't a case for me, after all. What if there was a supernatural at work? A ghost could have pushed the chief without him realizing what happened. Or maybe this Wade Cantrell was more than human. If so, then I needed to keep Chief Fox in the dark until I had more information.

"Thanks for your help, Chief," I said. "Hopefully, we can figure out what happened so you'll be able to cross over."

Chief O'Neill's gaze darted around the room. "Cross over to where?"

"To the next place," I replied. "Heaven, the underworld. Whatever that is for you. I don't know."

His expression became pained. "I don't know that I want to leave this town. It's been home for my entire life."

"Well, I'm not sure that you'll get to stay. It's likely the unfinished business that's keeping you here."

The chief floated in a circle, wringing his hands. "Do you have any pull? Can you keep me here?"

"Chief, you're dead," I said softly. "Whatever's waiting for you is going to be preferable to haunting Chipping Cheddar."

"I'm not so sure," he said.

I paused, thinking. "Tell you what. Let's solve the murder first, to put residents at ease."

"Yes, that's important."

"Right. I thought you'd feel that way, having been the chief of police and all. And then we'll figure out what's next for you. Sound good?"

The chief nodded. "How about I go with you? I might remember something if I'm back at the scene of the crime."

I started. "You want to go to the marina?"

"Sure. I'm dead now. What harm can it do to be near the water?"

He had a point. "Okay, I'll meet you there." I had no idea how ghosts traveled, but I assumed he wouldn't be buckling in to my passenger seat.

I knew Chief Fox would be annoyed if he found out I questioned a suspect on my own, but he had no way of knowing about Wade Cantrell and I had no way of explaining to him how I identified him as a suspect. 'I spoke to the victim's ghost' didn't seem like the ideal answer.

I left the kitchen and returned to my car. I'd never met Wade Cantrell and didn't know what to expect, but it didn't bode well that Chief O'Neill disliked him. He liked everyone he met. He could've been the mayor if he hadn't been the chief of police.

I headed to the marina to find Wade, ready to judge for myself.

CHAPTER ELEVEN

LIKE HIS YACHT, Wade Cantrell was hard to miss. He wore Gucci sunglasses and slides with his coral, knee-length shorts and a white polo shirt. His brown hair was perfectly coiffed and his tan likely never faded. He would have looked more at home in Palm Beach than Chipping Cheddar.

"Excuse me. Are you Mr. Cantrell?"

He flipped up his shades for a better view of me. "For you? Definitely."

Oh boy. I fixed him with a bright smile. "Great. My name is Eden Fury and I was hoping you could answer a few questions for me."

"Would love to. Care to ask them on my yacht over a few drinks?" He lifted a suggestive eyebrow.

Why not? It might loosen his lips and I could take care of myself. "On a hot day like today? That sounds delightful."

He beckoned me forward and I dutifully followed. I had no doubt this guy took bubble baths with his sunglasses on. Probably took selfies of it, too.

I had to admit—the yacht was impressive. "This is amazing," I cooed. "I can't imagine owning something as spectacular as this. You are one lucky guy."

His lips melted into a seductive smile. "I could be luckier."

Creep.

"Allow me to get you a drink." He went below deck and returned a minute later with two flutes.

"Prosecco?" I asked, accepting the glass.

He gave me a tart look. "Champagne."

I sniffed it to see if I could identify any drugs he may have slipped in. He struck me as the type. His defense would undoubtedly be that he was so wealthy and fabulous that he didn't need to resort to drugs to get a girl in bed. As though that was the issue. Thankfully, the champagne looked and smelled clean.

I took a sip. "Mmm. Bubbles are the best. I like everything fizzy."

"You seem plenty bubbly yourself," he said. "I like a woman with energy."

I moved to the edge of the deck, partially for a view of the water and also to be seen by passersby in case Wade decided to push me overboard or worse.

"This is a wonderful view," I said.

"It certainly is." He joined me, downing his drink in one gulp.

I didn't sense anything supernatural about him. If he was responsible for the chief's death, then he was sneaky about getting him in the water.

"So what questions do you have for me?" Wade asked. "Are you a journalist? I've been featured in Yachters Monthly."

"Have you?" I tried to sound impressed.

His smug expression told me I was successful. "It takes real balls to sail around the world."

I never understood that expression—the use of balls to denote toughness or resilience. Balls didn't push out babies the size of a watermelon. Balls didn't feed hungry infants in the middle of the night. I figured Wade wouldn't appreciate my diatribe on balls, so I simply said—

"Wow." I sipped again.

"I know, right? You haven't seen a sunset until you've seen it from the other hemisphere."

I was pretty sure it looked the same, but he seemed relaxed enough to get started, so I did. "I understand that you had a heated debate with Chief O'Neill last week."

He clenched the stem of his flute. "How did you hear about that?"

"Oh, you know how the rumor mill is in this town. Always working overtime."

"I don't actually," he said. "I tend to spend most of my time here on the yacht."

"Then why be here at all?" I asked.

"It's a picturesque place from this vantage point." He swept his arm toward the shoreline. "Not as pretty as Monaco or Capri, but it has its charms."

"So what was the argument about?" I pressed.

"He tried to issue me a ticket for reckless driving," Wade complained. "I don't need that on my record."

"Were you?" I asked. "Driving recklessly?"

"I might go a little faster than the speed limit, but how is that any different from driving in a car?"

I peered at him. "People driving in a car get tickets, too."

"Only if they get caught."

"Um, you got caught."

Wade looked at me askance. "Whose side are you on?"

I didn't know how to answer that without getting booted off the yacht, and I wasn't finished asking my questions. "Did you end up getting the ticket? I bet you didn't." I nudged his arm playfully.

"I did, as a matter of fact, and I wasn't happy about it."

"How unhappy were you?"

He frowned. "What kind of question is that?"

"Unhappy enough to toss him overboard?"

"It was a citation, not a prison sentence."

"Okay, so maybe it was an accident that you tried to cover up," I said. "It's understandable. He's the chief of police and he's drowning. You're afraid if you try to save him, you'll drown too. People panic in that situation. It's a normal reaction."

"I did not panic," he griped.

"Oh, so you're saying you remained calm while the chief fought for his life in the water?"

"That is not at all what I'm saying," Wade said. His face was pink with pretentious rage.

"What happened after he issued the citation?" I asked.

"I yelled. He stayed annoyingly calm. He left the yacht. That's it."

"That's it?"

"Yes."

"You didn't leave the yacht to follow him?"

"No, I went downstairs to rejoin my special guest."

Ugh. "Who was your companion?"

He looked blank for a moment. "Lila. No, Leila. It was Leila."

Poor Leila. "Is she local?"

"Yes, I met her on the promenade the evening before. She'd been jogging and twisted her ankle."

"And you nursed her back to health with a few glasses of champagne and a good night's sleep?"

He smirked. "It was a good night. Can't comment on the sleep."

I heaved a weary sigh. "Any idea where I can find her? Maybe a last name?"

"No idea about her last name. She said she works at the diner. Gouda Nuff."

In that case, Leila would be easy enough to track down. "And what did you do after she left?"

"I showered and then I called my mother to complain about the citation."

"You called your mom? What are you, five?"

Wade sulked. "She was appropriately outraged."

And I'm sure she shoved a few grand into his trust fund to ease his pain. "What time did you speak to her?"

He pulled out his phone and tapped the screen. "It was early. I know that much. She chastised me for interfering with her beauty sleep. Mother doesn't function without her full eight hours."

He turned the phone toward me so that I could see the time stamp.

"And what did you do after you cried to mommy about receiving that well-deserved citation?"

He snatched the flute from my hand, clearly irritated that he'd wasted his good champagne on me. "I went to breakfast at The Daily Grind. They serve the only drinkable coffee in this town."

Well, we agreed on that score.

"Who waited on you?"

"Caitlin."

I started, not expecting he'd know the answer. "You actually take time to learn their names?"

"Only the pretty ones," he admitted.

Jerk. Part of me was tempted to sprout my wings and frighten him overboard.

"I'm going to check out your alibi. Assuming it matches

your story, you might want to think about relocating this yacht somewhere else," I said.

His gaze swept across the deck. "Why would I do that?"

I patted his cheek. "Because Wade, my love, there's a new chief in town."

Clara sat across from me in the Gouda Nuff diner. Every sip she took of her chocolate milkshake made my stomach sick with envy. It didn't help that she had a plate heaped with bacon and a stack of silver dollar pancakes. That's the beauty of diners—you can eat whatever you want whenever you want.

She smiled. "Eden, if you're hungry, order something."

"I already ate," I said. "I'm just here to check out Wade's alibi." I'd told Clara about speaking with the chief's ghost and my conversation with Wade Cantrell.

"But the way you're staring at my food…It's like your mother in front of a cosmetics counter."

I snorted. "What can I say? The woman loves her makeup."

"Who cares if you already ate?" Clara slurped the thick ice cream through her straw. "It's not like you're on a diet."

"And I'd like to keep it that way," I said. "If I keep eating the way I do, there will come a day when I start gaining weight." And I'd be terrible at trying to lose it. I had discipline, but not when it came to good food.

Clara speared a piece of bacon with her fork. "Eden, is anyone in your family overweight?"

"No," I said slowly.

"Do you live a sedentary lifestyle?"

"No."

"Then what makes you think you're going to be overweight?"

"I don't want to buy new pants." Ever. I also had no idea whether my family members used magic to stay slender. They'd never admit it if they did, which meant my real genetic disposition was a mystery.

Clara waved to the waitress. "Leila, can we please get another chocolate shake?"

Leila snapped her gum. "Sure thing. Anything else?"

"As a matter of fact, there is," I said. I lowered my voice so as not to be overheard by the people in the booth behind us. "Do you know Wade Cantrell?"

"Sure. We've met," she said, smiling.

"Is it true that you spent the night on his yacht recently?"

Leila glared at me. "Are you trying to slut shame me or something? Because we're both single adults…"

I held up a hand to stop her. "Not at all. Were you on the yacht when Chief O'Neill issued Wade a citation?"

"I was below deck, but I heard their conversation. Wade got a little loud at one point, but he cooled." She ran her tongue across her upper lip. "Then when he came back down to me, he got hot and bothered all over again."

"On second thought, I don't think I need that milkshake."

"Any more details you'd like to know?" Leila asked, clearly enjoying my discomfort.

"Do you remember whether Wade came straight down after the chief left?"

She nodded. "Sure did. I heard him call the chief a name over his shoulder on the steps. He wanted to have the last word."

Naturally.

"He told me the chief seemed to be afraid of the water," Leila said. "He thought it was funny. I told him I didn't find it funny at all because I have a real fear of butterflies. If someone stuck me in one of those butterfly gardens, I'd have a heart attack."

Ugh. Laughing at the chief's deep-rooted fear of water? I really hoped Wade took his yacht and hightailed it back to whatever port he came from. "And you're sure you didn't hear a splash?"

Leila narrowed her eyes. "Hang on. Are you asking me all these questions because you think Wade pushed the chief into the bay and drowned him?"

"I'm simply following up on a lead," I said.

"Why? Are you the new chief? I thought the new chief was hot."

"She's FBI," Clara interjected.

Leila's eyes flickered with surprise. "I see."

I flashed my FBM badge, which I knew would appear as a normal FBI badge to her. "Agent Fury."

"Well, Agent Fury, I think you're out of luck with Wade."

I thought so, too. "I appreciate your candor, Leila. If you think of anything, though, will you let me know?"

"Sure will." She snapped her gum again. "If you're not going to order anything else, are you ready for the check?"

Clara patted the table. "Leave it here, thanks."

Leila dropped the check and moved on to the booth behind us.

"What are you thinking?" Clara asked.

"What do you mean?"

"You have that look." Clara tried to imitate my expression by scrunching her face. "It means your brain is hard at work."

I knew I had an expressive face, but I didn't realize it was *that* transparent. "Well, a thought did occur to me. The thing Leila said about the butterflies."

"I know. I didn't realize fear of butterflies was an actual thing."

"It is. Lepidopterophobia."

"So why is that relevant?"

"Paul Pidcock died from his allergy to bee stings. If you

know you have a severe allergy that can kill you, you're probably afraid of bees, right?"

"I know I would be."

"And Elliott Bradford had a fear of enclosed spaces. Avoided them at all costs, but for some reason, felt compelled to take the elevator and had a heart attack."

Clara's brow creased. "You think they're all related."

"I'm starting to think so. Chief O'Neill doesn't remember anyone near him or pushing him, but he remembers feeling compelled to go to the water. What if Elliott felt that same compulsion to go into the elevator? And why Paul approached an active beehive?"

Clara shivered. "You think a demon is responsible?"

"I think it's highly likely." Many demons, like my father and brother, draw power from their victims. It was possible that whatever demon was on the loose in Chipping Cheddar was absorbing the fear of their victims. Fear is one of the strongest emotions and can create powerful energy.

"Why haven't you seen their ghosts?" Clara asked.

"The other two victims?"

"Yes. If Agent Pidcock was murdered by the same demon as Chief O'Neill, wouldn't his ghost be haunting your office?"

"Not necessarily," I said. "Paul was a wizard. He doesn't necessarily stick around if things go south for his body."

"Can you summon his ghost?" Clara suggested. "He'd be more aware of an invisible demon hand than humans like Chief O'Neill or Elliott."

"Good point." Although summoning someone like Paul meant I'd need to enlist the aid of my mother's family. I didn't have enough experience to do it on my own.

Clara handed me a slice of bacon. "Fuel for thought."

"I love that you still eat bacon with a fork."

She chewed happily. "Old habits die hard."

Although it wasn't the lead I expected to uncover when I went to see Wade Cantrell earlier, a supernatural killer made a lot of sense. Unfortunately, it also meant that my role in the investigation was about to get a little tricky with Chief Fox.

CHAPTER TWELVE

My epiphany in the diner had me steeped in thought all the way home. I barely managed to get through the front door when Princess Buttercup accosted me.

"I'm sorry," I said, patting her head. "I've been out all day, haven't I?"

The hellhound's mournful expression told me that she was, indeed, feeling neglected.

"How about a nice walk around the neighborhood?"

Her tongue rolled out, sparks shooting along the way. One of the hazards of being a hound from the underworld.

"Eden, is that you?" My mother's voice rang out.

"Perfect timing," I whispered to Princess Buttercup. Loudly, I said, "I have to take the dog for a walk." I didn't manage to escape before she caught up with me.

"About time," she replied. "You can't keep a hellhound that size cooped up in the house all day. She needs fresh air and exercise."

"There's a house full of people here," I said. "Anyone could have let her out in the backyard."

My mother harrumphed. "She's your responsibility. Your

niece's snake and your grandmother's cat are more than enough for the rest of us to take care of."

Wait, what? "What snake?"

"Olivia's snake. Charlemagne."

"How have I not seen this snake?" I asked. I wasn't a huge fan of slithering critters.

"What do you look so nervous about?" my mother asked. "Your ancestors' hair was full of snakes. You're lucky you didn't inherit that trait."

My hand flew instinctively to touch my hair. "Definitely lucky."

"Charlemagne is a giant sweetie pie," my mother continued. "He's a reptilian puppy if ever there was one."

"You mean he pees in the house and chews your furniture?"

My mother narrowed her eyes. "No, I mean he chases the cat and likes to lick."

I cringed. "With a forked tongue? Gross."

Princess Buttercup whined beside me. She was desperate.

"I'll be back in twenty minutes," I told my mother.

"Good, because I need you to help me with..."

I put my hands against my ears and began to chant as I accompanied Princess Buttercup outside.

We walked to the corner of Munster Close and turned right onto Gruyere Way. The sun was still shining and it felt good to be walking at a brisk pace with Princess Buttercup by my side. For a moment, I was back in San Francisco, making my way down the crookedest street and laughing at the oversized vehicles that got stuck when they failed to properly navigate the street.

"Eden Fury, as I live and breathe."

Ugh. I didn't need to look to recognize that shrill voice. "Hey, Tammy." Tammy Leighton was probably in her mid-fifties but still wore her graying hair in pigtails.

"It's lovely to see you. Listen, dear, I know you haven't been here in quite some time, but you simply can't walk your hellhound off leash."

"Since when?" Tammy was a human with the Sight, so it didn't surprise me that she could see Princess Buttercup in her natural form.

"HOA rule number thirty-seven. Your parents have copies of the handbook if you need to familiarize yourself with the neighborhood rules now that you're back."

I stared at her. "When did the neighborhood form an HOA?"

"Three years ago," she said. "I'm the president, of course." She smiled like she'd won the Citizen of the Year award.

"Humans can't tell she's a hellhound, you know," I reminded her.

"It doesn't matter," Tammy said. "Great Danes need to be leashed all the same. Even my precious Captain America needs to be walked on a leash and he's not a threat to anyone."

Captain America was Tammy's dachshund. "He's still around, huh?" He had to be pushing the limits of his lifespan, bless him.

Tammy practically burst with pride at the mention of her beloved dog. "He's gone a bit gray around the face, but who hasn't?" She tittered. "He's still the same wonderful companion." Her hard lines seemed to soften. "Tell you what. Given that you're sort of a born-again resident, I'll let you off with a warning this time."

"Thanks, Tammy," I said.

"And tell your Aunt Thora that I've seen those lemon trees in her garden," Tammy said, all business once again. She clucked her tongue. "She knows full well those are not permitted under HOA rule number ninety-two."

There was an HOA rule dedicated to lemon trees?

"Why can't she have them?" Aunt Thora was obsessed with lemons. If she could be buried in a coffin with lemons that stayed fresh for eternity, she'd welcome death tomorrow.

"They attract unwanted pests and disease," Tammy said. "We have to keep such things under control or the entire community suffers."

Tammy's problem was that she wanted to keep everything under control, no matter how minute.

"I'll pass along your message." Thankfully, Aunt Thora didn't share the personality traits of the other female members of my family. In other words, she wouldn't hex Tammy for her simple, rule-abiding request.

"How long do you and your hound plan to stay with your family?" Tammy asked.

"I'm not sure," I replied. "I just started a new job and I've been focused on that."

"Well, between you and your brother's family and the animals, your mother is already in violation of several rules."

"What does the HOA care how many family members are living under one roof?"

Tammy looked at me like I was nuts. "If we don't care, who will?"

"No one," I said. "No one outside of the house should care. Besides, my brother's family is only there until their remodeling is finished."

Tammy pressed her lips together. "So I've been told."

What was that supposed to mean? I'd had my fill of Tammy. Fresh air and exercise were supposed to de-stress me, not trigger more.

"It was good to see you, Tammy."

"Remember," she said. "Leash the beast next time."

I guided Princess Buttercup back toward Munster Close, no longer in the mood for a walk. We made it back to the driveway when the sound of a car caught my attention. I turned to see a police car come into view and my heart skipped a beat. What was *he* doing here?

Chief Fox pulled in front of the mailbox and waved. I stood awkwardly on the lawn, uncertain what to do. Was he here to kick me off the case because I spoke to Wade Cantrell by myself? Did he figure out there was something strange about me or my family?

"Good afternoon, Eden." He swaggered up the driveway, looking every inch the chief that he was. And in those tight jeans, I mean *every* inch. His sea-green eyes gleamed in the bright sunlight. He was like watching a living, breathing magazine ad.

"What brings you to Munster Close, Chief?" As I took a hesitant step forward, Princess Buttercup came rushing past me and nearly knocked me off my feet. She lunged for Chief Fox, throwing her front paws on his shoulders and licking his face.

"Whoa," the chief said. Thankfully, he was laughing and not drawing his gun.

"Princess Buttercup! Get down this instant."

The hellhound dropped to the ground and gave me a guilty look.

"She's yours?" Chief Fox asked. He stroked the hellhound's head. "I've never seen a dog like this."

"She's a black and white Great Dane," I said. "She's a rescue."

He smiled at Princess Buttercup. "Really? I hate the thought of anyone abandoning a dog, especially one as awesome as this. They'd have to be crazy."

If only he could see her true form, I wondered whether he'd hold the same opinion.

"Where did you find her?" he asked.

His question took me off-guard. I couldn't exactly say, *as*

*a matter of fact, mere human who knows nothing about the super-
natural, I found her abandoned outside the entrance to the underworld. Funny story, that.*

"Um, San Francisco. I think someone found it hard to
keep a dog her size in an apartment in the city. Too many
trips down the emergency staircase."

"Their loss is your gain. So listen, I thought we could talk
about the investigation, seeing as how you've been interro-
gating suspects without me."

Crap on toast.

I grasped at an excuse. "I had a good lead and I thought it
was best to move forward…"

Chief Fox didn't let me twist in the wind. "Relax, Eden.
Why don't we go inside and talk?" He inclined his head
toward my neighbor's house. "Because I think we might have
an audience out here."

I followed his gaze to where Mrs. Paulson was pretending
to sweep her front porch at an awkward angle—an angle
clearly designed to maximize her eavesdropping efforts.

"Sure. Come on in," I said weakly. I couldn't decide which
was worse—having Mrs. Paulson eavesdrop or invite him
into my family's home. I ran through a mental list of
everyone in the house and what they were doing. As far as I
knew, no one was wreaking magical havoc right now.

I made sure to enter the house first and call out to anyone
within earshot. "Look who's here for a visit! Have you all met
the new chief of police?"

My mother darted into the foyer, wiping her hands on an
apron with the picture of a chicken that read *Wake Up, Moth-
ercluckers.*

"Welcome to Chipping Cheddar, Chief Fox. It's so lovely
to meet you." She halted in front of him, clearly taken aback.
"My, my. I wasn't expecting someone so youthful and
attractive."

Was my mother seriously trying to flirt with a guy half her age? Of course she was.

"Are those real muscles?" my mother continued.

I rolled my eyes. "No, Mom. They're fake muscles. He wears padding under his shirt to beef himself up."

Chief Fox snorted. "An unintended by-product of an active lifestyle, I'm afraid."

"Who's afraid?" Grandma shuffled into the room in her terrycloth robe and slippers.

"Grandma, why aren't you dressed?"

"I got dressed yesterday," Grandma said. "That's enough for one week."

A black cat leaped from a nearby ledge and used the chief's shoulder as a springboard to the floor. He reeled back, startled. The cat turned to hiss at him before running off.

"That's Candy," I said. "My grandmother's cat."

"Why does your grandmother's cat have a stripper name?"

"Stripper name?" I echoed. "Well, I guess it takes one to know one."

"Candy's not a stripper," Grandma said. "I suppose she might have been in her former life, but it's not something we talk about."

Chief Fox chuckled. "She's reincarnated, huh?"

"Hexed, more likely," Grandma said. "Not by me, though. It was before my time. Whatever happened, she's still bitter about it."

"Grandma," I said in a low, warning tone.

"Are you talking to me?" Grandma asked. She rubbed her ear. "You'll have to speak up. My hearing isn't what it used to be."

If she weren't so old and prone to broken bones, I would have kicked her in the shins to silence her. Thankfully, Chief Fox seemed to embrace her comments as the amusing yet mad ramblings of an elderly woman.

"I'm Sawyer Fox," he said in a loud, clear voice. "I'm the new chief of police."

"It doesn't get more impressive with volume," Grandma replied. She padded into the kitchen and I breathed a sigh of relief.

"Have you offered the chief a cold beverage?" my mother asked me. Her accusatory tone was evident to everyone within earshot.

"I'm fine, thank you," Chief Fox said.

"You certainly are." My mother actually batted her eyelashes like a Southern debutante in heat. It was embarrassing.

I steered the chief through the French doors and into the home office. "And you were worried about Mrs. Paulson eavesdropping."

"Looks like we might be interrupting the CEO hard at work," Chief Fox said. He jerked his head toward the desk where Olivia spun around in the swivel chair.

"Don't call me that," she said.

"A CEO?" Chief Fox queried. "But that's a good thing."

"Depends on your point of view." She grabbed the edge of the desk to stop herself from spinning. "Want to see my constipated face?"

Chief Fox cast a quick glance at me. "Uh, sure."

Olivia squeezed her eyes closed, scrunched her nose, and flapped her arms. Her bright blue eyes popped open for his approval.

"Nice," the chief said smoothly.

Olivia dashed from the room to torment someone else.

"Sorry about that," I said.

"Hey, it'd be worse if she were actually constipated."

Why did he have to be so charming? It wasn't fair.

"Important question." His gaze was fixed on something behind me. "Who owns the cardboard cutout of Fabio?"

Oh no. I craned my neck and saw the life-size cardboard cutout of Fabio, the model that graced the covers of many of my mother's romance novels.

"Eden brought that with her from San Francisco," my mother said from the doorway.

I whipped toward her. "What? I did not!"

My mother placed a placating hand on my arm. "Now, Eden. It's nothing to be embarrassed about. Sure, he's a little older but those chesticles *are* enticing."

"I'm not embarrassed," I began, but my mother smoothly interjected.

"Good, then that's the end of that."

My insides were on fire. Why was my mom refusing to take ownership of Fabio? She adored Fabio. She decorated him for holidays with a string of lights and a Santa hat at Christmastime and a giant pink heart T-shirt for Valentine's Day.

I steered Chief Fox out of the office and away from Fabio. "Anyway, it was kind of you to stop by."

"But I didn't actually get to talk to you about the reason I'm here."

I hesitated. "Can we talk outside? It's too noisy in here for me to concentrate."

"It's not noisy," Grandma yelled from across the room.

"Now you can hear?" I called back. This family was maddening.

I marched outside with the chief right behind me. I dropped down on the front porch swing, making sure the door was firmly closed behind us.

"The coast is clear," I said.

"Your family is…interesting," he said.

"They're something," I replied. "What's your family like?" I pictured them in matching khakis and loafers with colorful collared polo shirts. They probably took their Christmas card photos in November at the beach.

He shrugged. "Typical Midwestern, I guess."

Okay, scratch the part about the beach.

"Des Moines, Iowa born and bred."

I scrunched my nose. "Is that potatoes?"

"That's Idaho." He cracked a smile. "And Ireland."

"Germans?"

"That's Minnesota."

"Is it cheese? No, that's Wisconsin." As someone from a cheesemaking town, I knew my cheese states whether I wanted to or not.

"Corn," he finally said. "Iowa is known for corn."

"Right." I peered up at him. "So what brings you all the way to the East Coast? That's a big change."

"I wanted a big change," he admitted. "I love the water. I spent a lot of time on boats at the lake growing up."

"Sounds idyllic." Not like my childhood of demons and curses.

"Sometimes," he said. "Sometimes boring."

"Boring has its advantages," I said.

He joined me on the porch swing. "Says the woman who interrogated Wade Cantrell for no apparent reason. What made you do that?"

"He's an attractive guy," I said. "I just wanted an excuse to talk to him."

Chief Fox regarded me. "I wouldn't have pegged him as your type."

"You think you know my type? We've known each other for what? Five minutes?"

He rubbed his hands up and down his thighs. "I wasn't trying to be presumptuous."

"How did you find out I spoke to him?"

"Deputy Guthrie overheard Wade bragging to the cashier

at the liquor store that he'd caught the eye of the prettiest woman in town."

"And Sean assumed it was me?" That was a stretch. He'd always had a thing for Sassy.

"No, it was when Wade went on to say that the prettiest woman in town was batshit crazy and accused him of murdering Chief O'Neill. That's when Deputy Guthrie thought of you." Chief Fox eyed me expectantly.

"Tensions are running high since the chief died," I said. "Any woman could've accused Wade of that."

"Uh huh." He leaned back against the swing. "I really need to get one of these. It's very relaxing."

"I used to fall asleep out here in the afternoons when I was a kid. Grandma would come and whack me with the broom to wake me up."

"She couldn't just call your name? Maybe shake an arm?"

I shrugged. "She's prone to violence." And dark magic, but I'd keep that part to myself.

He inched away from me. "Hope it's not genetic."

"I'm a boring cyber crime agent, remember? They don't do violence." One little white lie never hurt anyone.

Chief Fox was silent for a beat. "So do you think he did it?"

"No," I said. There was no reason to keep playing the game if he didn't believe me. "I think he's awful, but I don't think he killed Chief O'Neill."

"Then I guess we need to keep the investigation going."

I shot him a curious look. "That's it? You're going to move on from Wade because I said so?"

"Any reason I shouldn't?"

I drew my knees to my chest. "No, I'm just surprised you have that much confidence in me. You hardly know me."

He pinned his blue eyes on me. "You don't get to be chief of police at my age without having a decent radar in place,

Agent Fury. You've got good instincts, I can tell. I'm going to trust them until you give me a reason not to."

"Any more leads?" I asked. I certainly wasn't about to share mine or the chief would be jumping on board with Wade's assessment of 'batshit crazy.'

"Not yet, but I'll let you know, as long as you promise to keep me in the loop on your end." He stood. "And, just for the record, even if Wade hadn't mentioned the part about the chief's death, I would've known he was talking about you."

"Because I'm batshit crazy?"

He grinned. "Sure. Let's go with that."

Without a backward glance, he walked down the front porch steps. I stared at his tight jeans as he crossed the lawn and returned to his car. If I'd known there'd be a guy like that coming to Chipping Cheddar, I might have stuck around.

"Eden!" My mother had opened the front window and poked her head outside. "I told you I needed help before you took the dog for a walk. Get in here, please."

I heaved a sigh. Then again, maybe not.

CHAPTER THIRTEEN

My mother's plea for help involved deciding whether a blue top or a red top best complemented her coloring.

"*This* is what you needed me for?" I asked. "How do you not know your best colors by now?"

My mother adjusted the hem of the red top. "Well, honey, you wouldn't understand. When they all look so darn good, it makes it hard to choose."

"Wear the red," I said. "It highlights the burning flames of hell in your eyes."

"Look at you, Eden. Being so sweet." She inclined her head. "What do you want?"

I told her about summoning Paul's ghost.

"So now you want to use us for our magic?" My mother placed a hand on her ample hip. "I thought you found our magic beneath your lofty ambitions."

I closed my eyes and struggled to maintain my composure. "This isn't about me, Mom. This is about trying to stop a killer before he strikes again. Who knows? If we don't identify him soon, you could be next." Gods be willing.

My mother huffed loudly. "Fine, but I expect something

in return. We're not performing magical monkeys, not even for family. It takes a lot of time and effort…"

I knew her speech could go on for a while, so I caved immediately. I didn't have time to bicker. "I have an expense budget," I said. Maybe. I'd have to ask Neville.

My mother perked up. "Ooh, look at you, Miss Big Spender. Holding the FBM by the short and curly purse strings. Must be nice."

"No black magic," I added quickly. "Just a garden variety summoning spell."

Her brow lifted. "Now you propose to tell me how to do my own magic?"

"There's no need for blood or anything else," I said. "This kind of spell doesn't require it."

"You telling me what I can and cannot do under my own roof, young lady?"

"Do I need to show you my badge?"

We stared at each other for a lingering moment.

My mother broke first. "Fine, but only because it isn't necessary for the spell. One of these days, someone might remove that wand from your posterior and beat you with it."

I sighed. "Can we just get on with it?"

"I need Aunt Thora," she said. "We have to wait until she gets back from her gardening club meeting."

Now that I had a working theory, I didn't want to waste time. Not when there might be a demon killer on the loose. "Where's the meeting?"

My mother looked at me askance. "At the senior center. Why?"

"Because I'm going to get her," I replied.

"Great. Let's go," Grandma interjected. I didn't even notice her enter my mom's bedroom. For an old woman with creaky bones, she moved like a Ninja.

I whirled around. "There's no need for a passenger."

"You won't even know I'm in the car," she said. "I'll be as silent as the grave."

If only.

"Your idea of silence is banging pots and pans at a slow tempo."

Grandma laughed. "Play your music loud enough and you won't hear me. Oh, wait. You like that annoying noise that disguises itself as music. On second thought, I'll sing."

Dear gods of Olympus. "Grandma, I won't take you anywhere if you sing. You have to be quiet so I can think."

"Oh, is that the problem?" Grandma asked. "You mean if we'd have been quieter when you were growing up, you would've been smarter? Maybe you'd even have a full set of fury powers by now." She looked at my mother. "That's where you went wrong Beatrice."

"Oh, so this is my fault?" my mother shot back.

"I *am* smart," I said. "And I don't want those fury powers. You think I like having wings?" The words escaped my lips before I could stop them.

My grandma's eyes rounded. "You have wings? Since when?"

I groaned. There was no way I'd get out of this. "Since I left San Francisco. My...incident at work triggered a new fury trait."

Grandma clapped her hands. "Why didn't you tell us? This is great news. There's hope for you yet. Finally, your mother can stop casting her Lost Cause charm."

I froze. "Mom's been casting spells? About me?" I shot her an accusatory look.

"Don't worry about it," Grandma said. "She's been at it for years and you didn't notice."

"What do the wings look like?" my mother asked. "They're black, right? Please tell me they're black."

I closed my eyes, resigned to have the conversation. "Yes, they're black."

"How big is the wingspan?" Grandma asked. "Your cousin Stella grew wings that were six feet. I remember your father mentioning it once."

"Yours are at least that, right?" my mother urged.

"You're going to be competitive about wingspan, too?" I asked. "Is there anything you're not competitive about?"

My mother and grandmother exchanged quizzical looks. "I've got nothing," Grandma said.

"My wings are perfectly proportionate to my body," I said. I refused to give exact measurements.

They both scrutinized me. "Hmm," my mother said. "Maybe there's a spell..."

"Enough!" I said. "I need to get Aunt Thora." I yanked the door open and marched outside. Princess Buttercup was sprawled across the front porch and I nearly tripped over her. She lifted her head a fraction when she noticed me.

"You want to go for a ride?" I asked.

Her ears perked up.

"I'm not sharing a seat with that mutt," Grandma said. "She smells like acidic farts."

"You're not sharing a seat with her," I said.

"Good." My grandmother walked down the steps to the driveway and paused at the passenger-side door of my car.

"Because she's sitting in the front."

"Well, she's not sitting on my lap. I've already had two hip replacements."

"No, you're sitting in the back or you can stay here."

Grandma's eyes sparked with anger, but she opened the back door without another word. I opened the passenger door and Princess Buttercup came flying. She perched in the seat and hung her head out the window.

"Watch that slobber of hers," Grandma said. "She might burn people as we drive by."

"Buttercup doesn't slobber," I objected.

"Oh, so she has issues with her sweat glands then? I'm sure Verity can write a prescription for that."

I ignored her and focused on the road.

"Is this car cursed?" Grandma asked.

I glanced at her in the rearview mirror. "No, why?"

"Then why doesn't it go over forty miles an hour?"

"Because I'm in a twenty-five mile an hour zone," I said.

"So what? You're a federal agent. You get special dispensation."

"There are families out walking," I said.

"Ten points for that kid in the vest." She clucked her tongue. "No parent in their right mind should dress a kid in a vest."

"It's not the kid's fault," I said. "You used to dress Mom in black lace dresses."

"And she loved it," Grandma shot back. "She felt like a Head Priestess in that dress. Maybe if we'd dressed you in more black outfits, you'd have come around."

My gaze flicked to the mirror. "You really think my lack of black clothing is what ruined me?"

"No, I think your parents are what ruined you."

"I'll be sure to let them know you said that." I turned into the parking lot of the senior center. "We're here," I said, happy to change the subject.

"Use the handicapped spot," she said.

"I can't do that. I don't have a sticker."

"I'm your sticker."

"Grandma, you're not handicapped."

"Fine, then get one of your golf clubs out of the trunk."

"I don't have any golf clubs." I paused, the realization dawning on me. "Why do you need a golf club?"

"It'll help with the handicap issue."

"I'm not going to whack you in the knees with a club," I said, exasperated.

"I wasn't thinking of whacking me."

Argh. "This spot is perfectly fine."

"I'm an old woman. I can't walk all the way to the building from here."

"You don't have to," I said. "You can wait in the car with Princess Buttercup." I exited the car before she could object and ran into the building like it was on fire. Only after exploring every room of the senior center did I discover the gardening club met outside in the garden. Duh.

"So if you'll excuse Thora, she needs to come with us due to a family emergency." Grandma stood in the middle of the gardening circle, authoritative hands on hips.

Aunt Thora rose to her feet with the help of a friend. "No need to be dramatic, Esther. If you need me at home, just say so."

"We need you at home for a very special purpose that only you can..."

I cleared my throat. "That's enough, Grandma."

The entire gardening club had stopped whatever they were doing to stare at us.

"Eden Fury, are you back home?" an elderly man asked.

"Yes, Leroy. I told you she was," Aunt Thora said gently.

"It's nice to see you, Leroy," I said.

Grandma ushered Aunt Thora away from the circle. "You can practice being polite another time. We've got business to conduct."

We walked around the outside of the building and back to the car.

"What's the emergency?" Aunt Thora asked. "We were just about to discuss different types of tomatoes. I love tomatoes, not as much as lemons, of course."

"We can discuss tomatoes all the way back to the house," Grandma said. "Now get in the car."

Aunt Thora slid in the backseat with Grandma. Princess Buttercup was exactly where we'd left her. I had no fear of anyone trying to take her, not at her size.

I explained the situation as we drove to the house and Aunt Thora's expression grew brighter and brighter.

"We haven't summoned a ghost in decades," she said. "Remember the last time, Esther?"

"I remember," Grandma said. "We wanted to know where Uncle Amos had left his stash of homemade gin. Supposedly, he had barrels of it hidden somewhere in town."

"In Chipping Cheddar?" I asked.

"No, of course not. Uncle Amos never lived in this world. Otherworld."

"And he made gin?" I queried.

"Nothing like you've ever tasted," Grandma said. "Potent stuff."

"And you wanted it?" I asked. Badly enough to summon his ghost?

Grandma squinted at me. "Maybe you're not the only one who likes to drink and cozy up to strippers."

My face grew warm at the reminder of Chief Fox. "Do you remember how to summon a ghost?"

"What do you need us for, Eden?" Aunt Thora asked. "Aren't ghosts one of your specialties?"

"Not all of them," I replied. "And Paul wasn't human. Who knows where his shade ended up?"

"We can do this," Grandma said firmly.

I pulled into the driveway and we hustled into the house. My mother was already in the process of gathering the necessary items.

"What's the excitement?" Alice asked, swooping into the kitchen. "I sense a flurry of activity."

"We're summoning a ghost," I said.

"One's not enough?" Alice asked.

"Ghost," Ryan repeated. He sat in a highchair at the table, playing with...

"Ryan!" I snatched the knives off the table. "Mom! Do you not pay attention? Ryan had three knives."

My mother looked at me like I was on hallucinogens. "Who do you think gave them to him?"

"Verity would spit fire if she saw her son playing with knives."

"If Verity spit fire, I'd finally be impressed by your brother's choice in wives." My mother gave me a pointed look.

"Who's going to watch Ryan while we attempt the summoning?" I asked. Anton and Verity were at work and Olivia was at a play date, not that we'd ask a child to watch a child. Well, my mother would.

"Ryan is fine," Grandma said.

"What about Sally?" I suggested.

"Sally's not remotely fine," Grandma replied.

I huffed. "To watch Ryan!"

"I would be happy to keep an eye on the boy." Alice materialized in the chair next to Ryan.

"You don't mind?" I asked.

Alice gazed fondly at Ryan. "It's been quite some time since I've been able to enjoy the company of children."

"Just make sure he doesn't get into any trouble," I said, "and if he cries, come get me."

Alice nodded, but her gaze was planted on my nephew as he babbled to himself and piled his blocks one on top of the other.

I let my family members amass the rest of the materials they needed and followed them outside to the backyard. I watched as Grandma marched over to the fence and levitated to see over the top.

"Grandma, what are you doing?"

"Pipe down," she called over her shoulder. "I'm making sure that nosy Mrs. Paulson isn't pretending to weed her flowerbeds." Grandma returned to the ground and our group.

"What makes you think she's only pretending to weed?" I asked.

"Have you *seen* her flowerbeds?" Grandma said. "Looks like King Kong and Godzilla used them as a wrestling mat."

"They're in the privacy of her backyard," I noted. "How can you see them?"

Grandma gestured to the fence. "Weren't you paying attention? I just showed you how I see them."

"Right, and Mrs. Paulson's the nosy one," I muttered.

My mother finished lighting the candles. "Now we join hands."

"What good are the candles?" Grandma asked. "It's daylight."

"I admit, odds of summoning a ghost is usually best after dark, but we need to act now," my mother said. "Eden thinks time is of the essence."

"A demon has likely murdered three people in town so far," I said. "Yes, I think time is of the essence."

We all stood in a circle and held hands.

"Repeat after me," my mother said.

"Why you?" Grandma asked. "You're not the oldest. You're not even the second oldest."

My mother looked aggravated. "I'm just trying to get this show on the road. Why are you being difficult?"

"It's in my nature," Grandma replied. "Like excessive body hair is in your nature."

My mother's jaw tensed. "My body hair is perfectly normal."

"Now that you apply that special lotion Thora made." My grandmother smiled. "Don't think I don't know about that."

"Could we get started?" I asked. "I could really use Paul's help."

"Repeat after me," my mother said again with a sharp look at Grandma. "Underworlds, hear our call."

"Underworlds, hear our call," we said in unison.

"Earth, wind, fire, and air. The elements are ours to command," she said, and we repeated it.

"We ask that you bring forth the wizard Paul Pidcock."

I heard my grandmother emphasize the latter part of Paul's surname. Very mature.

"Come into the light," my mother said.

"Come into the light," we said in unison.

I watched expectantly, but nothing happened. No ghost materialized. The candles continued to burn. The wind didn't even blow.

"I feel resistance," my mother said, confused.

"You must be doing it wrong," Grandma told my mother.

"That's your answer?" my mother shot back. "It didn't work, therefore, I must be doing it wrong? When's the last time you performed a spell like this? Prohibition?"

Grandma scowled. "When's the last time you did? When you wanted a date on a Friday night?"

They locked eyes and Aunt Thora and I released their hands so we could put distance between us. No need to get caught in the crossfire.

"Maybe it's not working because the moon isn't visible," Aunt Thora said.

"Maybe it's not working because Eden isn't a full witch," Grandma said.

I balked. "Now you're blaming my genetics?"

Grandma shrugged. "Why not? We blame genetics for your moody disposition."

I studied the materials on the ground and contemplated the spell.

"Uh oh. She's thinking." Grandma took a step backward. "Watch out for shrapnel."

"What if someone's blocking our access to Paul's ghost?" I asked, ignoring her. "Is that possible?"

My mother frowned. "I guess if the killer knows what we are and that we might try to communicate with the deceased, then they could interfere with contact."

"How?" I pressed. "Can any supernatural do that or would it have to be a certain type?" And how would the demon know who we are and what we're capable of?

"We should try again tonight," my mother said. "When the moon is high."

"I don't think the moon is a factor," I said, understanding settling in. As a matter of fact, there was a demon in town that knew exactly who we are and what we're capable of. "I think you're right about the spell being blocked."

My mother straightened, pleased to be right.

"What will you do now, Eden?" Aunt Thora asked.

I glanced in the direction of my father's house. "I think it's time to practice the art of confrontation." And thanks to my upbringing, there was no magic required for that.

CHAPTER FOURTEEN

I saw Sally through the kitchen window and waved before opening the door.

"Hello, Eden," she said. "Care to join us for a drink? I was just opening a bottle of wine."

"No, thank you," I said.

My father and Gustav were in the living room, playing cards.

"Eden, you look wiped out," my dad said.

"Investigations can be exhausting."

"Any progress?" he asked.

"A bit," I said. "I've narrowed it down to a demon."

My father's curiosity was piqued. "You don't say."

I looked past him for a better view of his guest. "Gustav, how long have you been in town?"

Gustav hesitated. "A little over a week, I guess."

"Before I arrived home from San Francisco?"

My father's expression grew tense. "What are you asking, Eden?"

"I'm asking whether Gustav arrived in town before I did."

"Maybe he did," my dad said. "What of it?"

Gustav blanched. "What are you suggesting?"

"I think you know perfectly well what I'm suggesting."

My father pointed a menacing finger at me. "Don't start this, Eden. Just because Gustav is a demon doesn't mean he's guilty. Hell, if that's your attitude, then arrest your whole family. We're all responsible for Mick's death...and that other guy."

"Not just one other guy," I said. "Two other guys. Elliott Bradford *and* Paul Pidcock."

Gustav looked blank. "Who are they?"

"You don't need to know their names to be responsible for killing them," I said.

Gustav's cheeks turned crimson. "I don't kill anyone. That's not the kind of demon I am." A sheen of sweat formed across his brow. "I reap vengeance."

"Killing people using their worst fears against them qualifies as vengeance in my book."

"I'm like your dad," Gustav insisted. "Mine is never deadly."

I fixed him with a thousand yard stare. "You mean to tell me your vengeance has never resulted in death?"

Beads of sweat formed on Gustav's brow. "I specialize in financial setbacks. Bankruptcies, that sort of thing."

"People have killed themselves over less," I said.

"You think because he came from Otherworld that he's automatically a murderer?" my father asked. "What about Sally? Have you forgotten she and I met there?"

"When you were there on a business trip," I said. "Doling out revenge."

"You sound like your mother," my father said. "She hated all my traveling."

"It isn't the traveling I object to," I shot back. "It's the acts you perform when you get there."

"Gustav is not your guy, Eden," my father said. "No

suicides because someone couldn't make the mortgage payment. You said so yourself. Their worst fears killed them."

I searched Gustav's face for any sign of deceit, but I only saw an anxious demon—one that didn't want to be accused of a crime he didn't commit. I was at a loss for words. I believed Gustav and yet…It didn't make sense. It had to be him. It all fit.

The vein in my father's neck began to throb. "I'm tired of this argument, Eden," he said. "We are who we are."

"And I am who I am. That doesn't stop you from trying to drag me across the evil boundary line kicking and screaming."

My father ignored my remark. "Gustav wouldn't be responsible for the murders even if he was a killer."

I folded my arms. "Why not?"

"Because Chipping Cheddar isn't his territory."

"Why not cross into someone else's territory?" I said. "Isn't that a demon thing? Being bad? Breaking the rules?"

"We stick to a code," my dad said.

"You're demons with scruples now?" I threw up my hands and marched back into the kitchen where Sally was pouring three glasses of wine.

"Have a drink, Eden, darling."

Her perfume hung in the air between us. Sally loved her fragrances.

"I'm not in the mood."

"I can understand your desire for closure," Sally said. "Death is often a motivator for closure."

"It's not just closure, Sally," I argued. "People are dying. Good people."

The vampire put an arm around my shoulders. "You always cared too much. That's your problem."

I bristled. "I don't consider it a problem." I happened to think it was one of my better qualities.

"When I was a vampire back in Primrose Hill, I knew a young vampire named Rupert. Rupert fought his nature at every turn. He wouldn't drink blood. He tried to protest his family's feedings." She shook her head. "Rupert was a laughingstock in Primrose Hill."

"I wouldn't have laughed. He sounds like someone I would've liked."

"Exactly." Sally took a sip of wine. "Do you know what happened to Rupert?"

"He moved away and lived happily ever after?"

"No, he died of starvation. Do you know how hard it is for a vampire to die of starvation? How painful? The poor boy wasted away, all because he refused to embrace his true nature."

I shuddered. "This is a terrible story, Sally."

"Yes, it is. That's the point. Terrible things happen to so-called good people, or vampires in Rupert's case. Let that be a lesson to you."

"I'm not going to starve," I said. Not unless my grandmother was left in charge of the cooking.

Sally patted my arm. "You're a Fury, Eden, whether you choose to embrace it or not. Furies have been known to possess incredible powers. You should consider yourself lucky."

"Their powers involve the ability to torture. I don't want that."

"We all have the ability to torture, even regular humans. Based on stories your father told me, that Tanner Hughes tortured you. Maybe not physically but emotionally. I don't think one is much worse than the other."

"Tanner is a jackass," I said. An attractive jackass, but a jackass nonetheless.

"I think maybe you should focus your efforts elsewhere.

This job—it just seems to exacerbate your vendetta against your family. It upsets your father."

"I don't have a vendetta against my family."

"Then maybe stop acting like you do. You're home now, Eden. Try letting go of all that virtue. See how it feels."

"I'll take it under advisement." I went back to the living room with my tail between my legs. "I'm sorry I accused you of murder, Gustav."

He waved a hand dismissively. "Water under the bridge. I've been accused of worse."

Worse than murder? I decided not to ask.

"You're going?" my father said. "No more accusations to throw around?"

"I promised I'd do bath and bedtime with Olivia and Ryan."

My father snorted. "Good luck with that." His tone was more ominous than I would've liked.

"It's a bath and then a bedtime story," I said. "How hard can it be?"

My father tried to cover his smirk with his cards. "For a talented agent like you, Eden? I'm sure it'll be a piece of cake."

"Olivia, please get in the tub," I commanded.

"I am not getting in there with my *brother*," she insisted.

"Duck," Ryan said. "Quack."

"You're little kids," I said. "It's a bath, not a marriage ceremony."

Olivia shrieked in protest.

"Fine," I huffed. "Give me a minute with Ryan, then you can take your turn."

"Quack," Ryan said.

"You want a duck?" I scanned the bathwater for a rubber duck but saw only an octopus, a mermaid, and a boat. At least they weren't encouraging him to drown sailors by using the mermaid as a siren.

"I want a shower," Olivia said. "And I can do it myself, thank you very much."

I cast a glance over my shoulder. Olivia was naked except for My Little Pony underpants. Her arms were crossed and her chin was lifted in defiance.

"It's hard to take you seriously right now," I said. "But you can have a shower. Satisfied?"

Olivia snapped the waistband of her underpants. "I hate these. Mommy bought them and says I have to wear them. Friendship and magic? Ugh."

I suppressed a smile. "What type of underpants would you rather wear?"

"Black, like my soul," she said.

I turned back to Ryan. "Alrighty then." Ryan laughed like I'd made the best joke in the world. "You're a good-natured fella, aren't you?"

"He caters to the masses," Olivia said. "It's pathetic."

"Nothing wrong with that." I felt something against my leg. I assumed it was the rubber duck and reached down to put it in the tub with Ryan.

It wasn't a rubber duck.

My scream pierced the air and Olivia began to laugh hysterically.

"That's Charlemagne," she said.

I backed against the wall and stared at the enormous snake. "What kind of snake is he?"

"A Burmese python," Olivia said. "He's my best friend."

"I can see why Pinky Pie isn't your idea of a good time." The snake was easily fourteen feet long with brown blotches and black borders.

Olivia dropped to her knees and stroked the snake's body. "He won't hurt you." She paused. "Unless you try to hurt me."

"You're my niece," I said. "I would never try to hurt you."

"Anton says you used to hurt him when he was a kid."

"That's a complete lie!" What a rotten brother. "Your dad used to torture me with nightmares." His demonic powers manifested early and he had no problem using them to practice on his little sister.

Olivia and Ryan both giggled.

The snake's tongue flicked out and he licked my bare leg. I cringed. "Would you mind steering Charlemagne into a larger room? The bathroom is a bit crowded."

"Let's go, Char," Olivia said. "Aunt Eden doesn't want to play with you right now."

Charlemagne ducked his head and swiveled around to leave, but not before opening his jaws to grab a squeaky toy that was hidden behind the wastebasket. The little round owl squeaked as the snake carried it out of the bathroom.

My heartbeat only slowed when Charlemagne was completely out of sight. I looked back at Ryan. "I hope you prefer hamsters when you're older."

"Charlemagne likes hamsters, too," Olivia said. "As a snack."

I choked on my own saliva.

Ryan spit water into the tub. "Fountain."

"Yes, you're a fountain. Congratulations."

"Will you show me your wings, Aunt Eden?" Olivia asked. "Pleeeease."

I jerked toward her. "Who told you about my wings?"

"I heard Great-Grandma and Mom-mom talking about it. They said you were ungrateful."

I turned back to shampooing Ryan's head. "I suppose I am, from their point of view."

"I would love wings," Olivia said. "But no one thinks I'm a fury."

"Sorry," I said. "Furies seem to be few and far between."

"I'll trade you," Olivia offered.

"It doesn't work like that," I said.

"Well, if you decide to fly one night, can I ride on your back?" Olivia asked. "I'm so small. No one will see me."

I glanced over my shoulder. My niece was so young, yet so eager to embrace the supernatural. I had no idea why I was so different, but I was.

"Sure," I said. I thought of my effort to rescue Chief O'Neill from the water. "I should probably practice using them anyway, just in case I ever need them in an emergency."

Olivia jumped up and down and clapped her hands. "I promise I'll stay quiet and out of sight."

I laughed as I rinsed Ryan's hair. "We'll both have to do that. We can't let humans see me with wings, remember?"

"If I had wings, I'd wear them for show-and-tell," Olivia said.

"You'll have to settle for a painting you drew over the weekend, I'm afraid."

She scrunched her nose, weighing the unfairness of my statement. "My turn for a shower."

I leaned over the bath to drain it. "Your sister's right, little man. Time to dry off."

Ryan stood up and by the time I reached for the towel, he was already dry. I blinked.

"How'd that happen?"

Olivia giggled. "Just a little magic, Aunt Eden."

"You can do that?" Wow. We were going to have to keep an eye on this one.

"I can do a lot more than that, but Mommy says I need a dope supervision."

"Adult," I corrected her.

"That's what I said!"

I lifted Ryan out of the tub. "Come on, Ryan. Let's get you

dressed and give your sister some privacy." Something my brother never gave me when I was younger.

"I'm glad you're here, Aunt Eden," Olivia said. "Mommom says you're a crap apple, but I like you."

"You mean a crabapple, and I like you, too." Maybe Clara was right. Maybe part of being here meant I could be a guiding light for my niece and nephew.

I picked up Ryan and began to exit the bathroom. Olivia swung the door closed too soon and it smacked me on the bottom. From the other side of the door, hysterical laughter erupted.

"Oops, sorry!" my niece called.

I rubbed the sore spot on my bottom and kept going. If I had any hope of influencing Olivia, I had a feeling my guiding light was going to need to shine like a supernova.

CHAPTER FIFTEEN

THE NEXT MORNING I decided to head into the office and discuss my theory with Neville. While we chatted, I set to work trying to tidy Paul's desk. No easy feat. The place was a mess.

"What's this, Neville?" I showed him a long stretch of paper with names, faces, and dates that was buried underneath a few folders.

Neville peered at the discovery. "The alerts from Otherworld. Our equivalent to the humans' wanted posters. Be on the lookout for any of those supernaturals. If you see them, you need to arrest them and send them back to Otherworld post haste."

I scanned the faces. No one looked familiar. "How often do these come in?"

"Every morning at ten," Neville explained. "No one's looked at them since Paul died, though."

"You didn't think this was important to mention?" It seemed like a necessary part of the job.

"I mentioned it now," Neville said.

I began tracking them back to the week of Paul's death. "Are you sure they come every day?"

"Yes, like clockwork. Sometimes Paul used the latest one as a dartboard. Chipping Cheddar isn't exactly a haven for demon fugitives. They're more likely to go somewhere they can blend, like a large city. Here, they would undoubtedly stand out."

Neville made a good point. "There's a date missing," I said. "The fifth. Any reason why it wouldn't be here?"

Neville's face turned ashen. "That's the day before Paul died."

I double-checked the stash of papers. Yep, the fifth was definitely missing. "I don't suppose you have any kind of security cameras set up in here?" Whichever demon was responsible, they knew enough to track down this office and hide evidence of their existence. Someone with a criminal track record made sense.

"No, infernal goddess," he said. "My surveillance is used on others, not us."

"You really ought to start locking the front door," I said, though a demon with the right skills could easily bypass a human lock. "Or maybe add a protective ward."

"I'll create one this instant." He moved to stand in front of the door and began to chant.

"Can we call a contact at Otherworld and get a copy of the missing alert?"

He stopped chanting and turned. "That should be easy enough," Neville said. "I'm happy to oblige you."

"Thanks."

"There." He dusted off his hands. "That should be sufficient." He headed back to his desk and the sound of a whistle set my teeth on edge.

"What's that, Neville?"

"I do believe the ward has been breached, darkest one," he replied sheepishly.

I bristled. "Will you please stop calling me names like that? I'm Eden or Agent Fury, if you want to be formal about it."

"But you're a rare and wondrous fury," Neville said, his voice a reverential whisper. "One that deserves the proper respect."

"I'm not dark. I'm not infernal. I'm certainly not wondrous." I clenched my fists. "I'm just a normal agent."

"And a pretty lousy one at that." My mother burst through the front door. "I breezed straight through your ward and nothing happened to me. Not even a little pinch."

My jaw unhinged. "Mom! What are you doing here?"

Neville held up a finger. "I'll make that call now." He took out his phone and moved to the back of the office.

"Your brother is at work and your father is out of town on a vengeance request, not that I dare ask that man for anything except a divorce," my mother said. "Anyway, I wanted to make tuna sandwiches for lunch."

"So make tuna sandwiches."

She thrust out a jar of mayonnaise. "I couldn't open this."

I gaped at the sealed jar. "You came all the way to my office so I can open a jar?"

"Who else? The rest of the family lacks your oversized hands."

"Mom, you can't just show up here. I don't work in retail. I'm an agent."

"I didn't come all the way here. I was planning to have a picnic nearby."

"In the park across the street?"

"Of course not. In the cemetery around the corner. Ryan is in the car."

My eyes popped. "You left a one year old unattended in the car?"

She waved a hand airily. "I put a ward on the car." She glanced back at Neville. "And it's a lot stronger than the one you had here."

I groaned. "Mom. You can't take Ryan on a picnic in the cemetery. People will notice."

"What do I care what people think? I used to bring you and your brother there all the time. You loved talking to the ghosts."

That was before I knew how weird it was for other people to see me talking to the air.

I opened the jar and handed it back to her. "Don't do this again. I'm very busy."

"Yes, yes. You and your important work eradicating evil." She continued to stand there, holding the jar.

"What?"

My mother bit her lip. "You can't date him."

"Who?"

"The new chief."

"Who says I want to date him?" I asked.

"Oh, please. I want to date him and he's not even my type."

"Handsome and funny isn't your type?"

"Well, you've seen your father," she replied.

"Not saying that I want to, but why would you possibly disapprove of the chief of police?"

"You know why," she said pointedly. "He doesn't *do* anything."

"Doesn't do anything? He's the chief of police in Chipping Cheddar. A very young chief, I might add."

She blew out a dismissive breath. "That's nothing. Anybody can do that."

ANNABEL CHASE

"Mick O'Neill wasn't just anybody," I said. "He was our friend."

"Don't put words in my mouth. You know that's not what I mean. Chief Fox is pure, unadulterated human. Getting involved with someone like him is a recipe for disaster and you know it."

"I'm not involved with him," I said.

"Good, then let's keep it that way." She gave me a hard look. "You'd compromise your whole family in a relationship like that."

"And I don't compromise the family in a job like this one?"

"That's to be determined." My mother wiggled the mayonnaise jar. "Thanks for your help." She turned around and waltzed out the door.

Neville waited until the door was closed to approach me. "A formidable woman, your mother."

"An inherited trait."

"I can see that." He handed me his phone.

I squinted at the screen. "What am I looking at?"

"The missing alerts from the fifth," he replied. "I was able to download them."

I swiped through the faces. It was like Tinder for ugly people. Unsurprisingly, Gustav's face was not among them.

"Recognize anyone?" I asked.

Neville studied the images over my shoulder. "No, O bright and fiery one."

"I'm going to bright and fire you in about two seconds," I threatened.

Neville ducked his head. "I will endeavor to be worthy of you."

"You don't have to be worthy of me. We work together. You're my trusted assistant, as in I trust you to stop the worshipping. It's weird."

"As you wish."

"I do wish." I examined the alerts more closely. "A warlock with a racketeering conviction. A vampire with a bloody trail." I shuddered, thankful that my own vampiric family member preferred her blood out of a bottle. "Great balls of fury!"

"What is it, my beatific…What is it, Agent Fury?"

"This guy." I tapped the screen. He was as ugly as they come, with bumps and scales and two holes that passed for a nose. If Voldemort and a dragon had a baby, it would be this guy.

"He'd be impossible to miss in Chipping Cheddar," Neville said. "If he were responsible for the murders, we most certainly would have seen him."

"No, Neville, we wouldn't have," I said. "Read the fine print."

Neville concentrated on the tiny paragraph at the bottom of the screen. "He was eviscerated. His shade escaped a maximum security holding cell." He gasped. "He could be right here and we wouldn't even know it."

"He is here, Neville, and we do know it." My jaw tightened. "And I think I know where to find him."

"We've already been down this road, Eden," my father said sharply. "Gustav had nothing to do with those murders."

I stood in my father's living room with a printed image of the suspect.

"I'm not here for Gustav," I said. "I'm here for this guy." I shook the paper. "His passenger."

Gustav scrutinized me. "My what?"

"Your passenger. Also known as a hitchhiker. When you came through the Otherworld portal in New York, you didn't come alone."

Gustav shook his head. "Of course I did. I think I would know if I brought someone through with me."

"Not if the hitchhiker wasn't corporeal," I said.

My father sucked in a breath. "A demon shade. How did you figure it out?"

I explained about the missing alert. "Once I saw that he was invisible, I realized what likely happened. Last night Olivia asked to go flying with me. She said she'd stay hidden on my back because she was so small. And the other day Grandma wanted to hitch a ride to collect Aunt Thora from her gardening meeting. She promised to stay quiet."

My father's laughter interrupted me. "I can imagine how that went."

"That's what made everything click into place," I said. "She couldn't be quiet if her life depended on it." She even upstaged me at my own dance recital when I was nine. You would think she'd use her magic to help her granddaughter nail the moves, but no. My grandmother used her magic to help Grandma nail the moves—right in front of the stage for all to see. She stole the show. Clara and I spent the next week hiding in the bathroom at school so kids didn't make fun of me. She was a good best friend, that Clara. I was an idiot for distancing myself from her all these years.

My father shrugged helplessly. "You know your grandma. She needs to be seen."

"Why haven't you seen him?" Sally asked.

"I don't see shades or ghosts that don't want to be seen," I explained. "If Alice wants alone time, she disappears from my sight." I sucked in a breath. "Anyway, he's a fear demon. He used the victims' fears against them."

"That's why there was no physical evidence," my father said. "He didn't lay a finger on them. He didn't have to." He looked a little in awe of the fear demon.

"But the scanners at the portal..." Gustav scratched his

head. "They should have detected another demon." His expression shifted, a spark of memory.

"What do you remember, Gustav?" I asked.

He hesitated. "There was a glitch," Gustav said. "When I went through the scanner, it froze. They had to send me through again. I thought it was because of the ceramic dragon."

"The demon probably attached himself to someone else on the other side of the scanner and then reattached to you when you walked through," I said.

Gustav's brow knitted together. "He can do that?"

"Absolutely," I said. "His whole plan was likely to enter this world and feed off the fears of his victims until he gained strength."

"So I set him loose in Chipping Cheddar?" Gustav asked.

"I'm afraid so," I said. "He only needed to attach himself to you to get through the portal undetected."

"And then decided to travel a bit further with you," my father said. "Can't say I blame him, Gustav. You're good company."

"My guess is he's staying here until he can gain enough power to return to a corporeal state," I said.

"So you need to stop him before he returns fully to his physical form," Gustav said, understanding.

"Yes, based on what he's done so far with no body at all, he's a powerful demon," I said. "There's no telling what he'll be capable of once he's completely restored."

My father's gaze swept the room. "So the question is—where is he now?"

CHAPTER SIXTEEN

THE ATTIC WAS TOO dark for reading, so I squirreled myself away in the sunroom at the back of the house and hoped no one noticed me.

No such luck.

"What are you doing in here, Eden?" My mother stood in the entryway. She wore a shimmering black, knee-length dress with kitten heels. I had to admit, her legs still looked as good as ever. Probably a spell. The woman would only run if chased and, let's face it, no one was foolish or brave enough to chase her.

"Research," I said. "Why are you dressed for one of Gatsby's parties?"

She pressed her palm flat against her chest. "If only. This is a date with a mere mortal. Bryant Pullman."

My eyes popped. "A date? You're dating?"

"Why wouldn't I?"

Because you're old didn't seem like the best answer. "I didn't realize that was something you did."

"Sweetheart, I've been dating since before you left town. You just were too wrapped up in your own world to notice."

Or maybe I didn't want to picture my mother giggling over tiramisu at the Chophouse.

"Wait. Why are you allowed to date humans, but I'm not?"

Her tinkling laughter filled the room. "Eden, I've had my children. I'm not looking for anything serious, just a bit of fun."

I did not want to picture my mother having fun of any kind, certainly not naked fun. "So who's Bryant Pullman?"

"You remember him, Eden. He taught at the high school."

"*Mr.* Pullman?" My whole body broke out in a sweat. "But he was my history teacher in eleventh grade." I remembered his pronounced Adam's apple and his enthusiasm for Teddy Roosevelt.

"And tonight maybe he'll manage to teach me a few things." She winked and I wanted to crawl under the wicker chair and die.

"Well, have a good time. Don't talk about me." I returned my focus to the text in my lap, but my mother wasn't finished torturing me yet.

"Sweet Hecate. Is that a book?" She practically recoiled.

"Yes, it's a book. That thing with pages and words that provides entertainment or information."

"You don't have to get smart with me, young lady. Have you forgotten the punishment for a sharp tongue around here?"

How could I? It used to involve a swollen tongue, so that no matter how I moved my mouth, my teeth ended up nipping the edges. Good times.

"Sorry, it's not a grimoire," I mumbled.

"Pfft. Who uses a grimoire anymore? If I want to learn a new spell, I go online."

I rolled my eyes. "Of course you do."

Not put off by the sight of a physical book, she came over to inspect it. "Your father will be pleased." She tapped the page I had open, where the face of a fear demon stared back at me. "Finally getting in touch with your demonic side?"

"It's for the case I'm working on," I said. "I need to learn as much about fear demons as I can."

"Or what will happen?" My mother suppressed a laugh. "You were always such a dramatic child. Everything was life or death with you."

I gaped at her. "This *is* life or death," I said heatedly. "It's the whole nature of my job."

She patted my shoulder. "Of course it is, dear."

"It's the nature of a lot of demons' jobs," Grandma interjected.

I jolted. I hadn't even noticed her snoozing in the chaise lounge on the other side of the sunroom.

"See?" my mother said. "You're not so different from the rest of us."

I wasn't in the mood to engage. "Fear demons grow stronger by feeding on the fears of their victims. A shade would need to absorb *a lot* of energy in order to return to his physical form."

"You think that's why Mick died?" my mother asked.

"Yes, I think the demon has been trying to suck as much fearful energy as he can in order to return to his natural state. It wasn't enough to scare Chief O'Neill with a fear of drowning, he had to take it as far as possible." Too far.

"Which resulted in Mick's death," my mother said. I was grateful to hear the note of sadness in her voice. It reminded me that my family wasn't all bad, even though it seemed that way to me most of the time.

"That would explain the elevator guy." Grandma snapped her fingers. "What's his name?"

"Elliott," I replied. "Yes, he had a fear of enclosed spaces. The demon likely sensed his fear and compelled Elliott into the elevator, then sucked the fear from him until he died of a heart attack."

My mother perched on the edge of the chaise lounge. "And Paul Pidcock, too. The bee sting allergy."

I nodded. "And the demon leaves no evidence because he has no physical form. Not yet." But he had to be close to regaining his solid form. "According to the book, once he's amassed the requisite level of energy, he needs to complete one final act."

"A ritual," my mother said.

"Yes. How'd you know?"

She patted her perfectly coiffed hair. "My brains are almost as big as my boobs."

I cringed. "Thanks for that mental image." I consulted the book. "I'm trying to find out what's involved so that I can get one step ahead of him."

My mother chewed her lip. "This might be more exciting than my date."

"You're going out with a high school history teacher," Grandma said. "A nap is more exciting than your date."

My mother twisted to glare at her. "I'll have you know Bryant is an absolute animal where it counts. It wouldn't surprise me to learn he's got some shifter in his bloodline."

I groaned. "Can we stop this conversation so I can get back to work?" If I could manage to focus after the image of Mr. Pullman as an amorous tiger assaulted my headspace.

My mother stood and smoothed the front of her dress. "You're such a child, Eden."

"Yes, *your* child," I said. "Which is why this discussion never needs to happen."

"You're just jealous because you're not getting any," Grandma piped up.

"Hey! Whose team are you on?" I demanded.

"The winning team." Grandma rested her head against the

pillow and closed her eyes. "Now if you'll excuse me, I'm rejoining David Hasselhoff in my dream. Word to the wise: a talking car is not the best place to get frisky unless you want a running commentary."

I smacked my head with the book. "I really need my own place." Like tomorrow.

"Your father and I were discussing that very topic," my mother said.

My brow lifted. "You were? And it was at normal volume?"

My mother smiled. "There was no yelling. It's nice when he and I can agree on a topic. Anyway, we've decided that, if you're interested, we can convert the old barn into separate living quarters for you. It's right on the property line so he and I needed to agree on it."

The old barn. "That's a decent size."

"We thought so," my mother said, clearly pleased with herself. "It would help you get back on your feet following your unfortunate…dismissal."

"I wasn't fired," I ground out.

"Why can't I have the barn?" Grandma asked.

A worthwhile question.

"Because I need to keep an eye on you," my mother told her. "Leaving you to your own devices hundreds of feet away is not a good idea for anybody."

Grandma waved a hand at me. "She's the one to worry about. I'm an old witch with barely passable skills. She's a fury."

"Whatever, Grandma," I muttered. "Why don't you put your passable skills to use and help me figure out how to stop this fear demon?"

"That's your job," Grandma replied. "I don't get paid for that."

I returned my attention to the book and tried to focus. "It

says here that in order to become corporeal, the demon will basically need to perform a ritual akin to summoning himself." I scanned the text. "He'll need the bay and the river."

"What about a pool?" Grandma said. "Josephine Levy has one. I wouldn't mind if he took shape there and then decided on a snack."

"Grandma!"

"What? She cheats at cards. I'm tired of losing."

"He needs the bay and river because he needs a vortex and that's the closest one," I said. A vortex is a place where multiple ley lines converge and powerful energy can be harnessed. I knew for a fact there was one in Chipping Cheddar. It would be impossible to house a portal to Other-world, dormant or not, and *not* have a vortex.

"A vortex makes sense," my mother agreed.

I snapped the book closed. "I'd better call Neville. I'm going to need his help."

"You're Eden Fury," Grandma said. "You don't need help from anybody, certainly not somebody called Neville."

"You need to embrace who you are, Eden," my mother chimed in.

"So what am I supposed to do if I run into the demon without a plan? Smite him?"

"You're not the hand of God, sweetheart," my mother said, patting my leg. "You don't smite."

That's where she was wrong. I was a fury. Smiting was in my DNA.

"Kill him and grind him into a fine powder," Grandma said. "I'll brew him in my tea."

I grimaced. "That's disgusting."

"You didn't complain when I made that nice lemon ginger concoction." She shuffled around on the chaise lounge until she seemed comfortable and closed her eyes again.

Okay, I was officially never drinking Grandma's tea again.

I jumped to my feet. "Thanks for the illuminating conversation, but I need to go." Now that I had the location of the ritual, I couldn't waste any more time.

My mother gave me an encouraging wave. "Good luck, dear. Have fun storming the summoning circle."

"Can you make me invisible?" I asked. Neville and I were in our office and I'd just finished updating him on my discovery.

Neville tilted his head. "You don't have the power of invisibility?"

"Not yet." And hopefully I never would. Invisibility would mean that I was on the path to full fury.

"Fascinating," he said. "I didn't realize that you acquire your abilities over time."

"It's because of my mixed bloodline," I said. "I have to demonstrate my aptitude for bad deeds and poof! I'm gifted a new skill." Like black wings for flying.

Neville shook his head. "Bad deeds. You've a warped sense of humor."

"What do you mean?" I swiveled my chair to face him.

"Furies aren't inherently evil," he said. "They simply mete out justice to evildoers."

"And revenge," I said. "They drive people insane. What if the person's crime was that he stole beef jerky from the convenience store? I don't think my type of justice is warranted in that case, do you?"

"You're afraid," Neville said quietly. "Be very careful, most malevolent mistress. You wouldn't want the fear demon using your energy to complete his transformation."

He had a point. I inhaled deeply. "I'm ready to take him

down, Neville. I've got a hemlock stick and I'm not afraid to use it, and an invisibility spell would help me out."

"A hemlock stick?" he queried. "To strike the death blow?"

"He was already eviscerated," I said. "It's not a moral issue." At least I didn't think so, but Neville's tone had me second-guessing myself. Good Goddess, a little over a week with my family and my moral compass was out of whack.

"I'll get straight to work on your charm." He stopped short. "What about the other items for the summoning circle? Surely, you need more than a hemlock stick."

I snapped my fingers. "Yes, can you also create a device that makes a supernatural appear human?"

"You already appear quite human," Neville said.

"It's not for me. Apart from that, I think I have what I need, except peppermint leaves," I said. According to the text, peppermint leaves were the best way to draw this particular demon to me. Any other time, my family had jars of peppermint leaves in the pantry because they were a common ingredient in potions and spells. Naturally, Aunt Thora had used the last of the leaves in a diaper rash potion for Ryan.

"I'm certain we can find an appropriate substitute if needed," Neville said. He spun around and vaulted himself toward the table at the back of the office. "Would you mind procuring a donut for me? Sugar helps me focus."

"Are you sure it doesn't have the opposite effect?"

"Quite."

Okay then. "Which kind?"

"Boston cream would be divine. Thank you."

I left him to work on my invisibility charm and went next door to Holes. The interior wasn't as downtrodden as I expected. In fact, it was downright adorable. Lots of bubblegum pink fixtures and fittings and shiny stainless steel. A plucky young brunette stood behind the counter wearing an apron covered in images of donuts.

"You must be Eden," she said with a big smile. "I'm Paige Turner."

"How'd you know?"

"I've seen you pass by with Neville and he mentioned a new boss." She frowned. "Losing Paul was a sad day for all of us. He loved his cinnamon donuts."

"Neville said you and your husband own this place."

She brightened at the mention of her husband. "We do! Some people think it's hard to work with your spouse, but Shia and I enjoy it. Plus, it was hard for him to find work because of his criminal record, so it was just easier for me to take him on."

Was it rude to ask about his record? Probably. "What was he convicted of?"

Paige's gaze darted around the shop, although there was no one else present. "Money laundering, but he's totally clean now, just like the money he laundered." She laughed awkwardly.

"Have you met the new chief?"

Paige leaned on the counter with a dreamy expression. "Have I ever? He likes bear claws and black coffee, in case you're wondering."

"Not wondering. Not even a little bit." I cleared my throat, trying to block the image of Chief Fox and I curled under a blanket in front of a crackling fire with a hearty breakfast of donuts and coffee.

Paige retrieved a Boston cream donut from the plastic compartment. "I know that's what Neville wants. How about you? Got a guilty pleasure?"

I examined the contents of the compartments. "I'll try a glazed chocolate, please." We'd have to relocate the office if I hoped to stay slim.

Paige produced a glazed chocolate donut. "Anything else? Coffee or tea?"

I suddenly remembered the need for peppermint leaves. "Do you happen to have any peppermint?"

"Like actual peppermint? How about spearmint gum?"

"No, that won't work. It has to be peppermint." Did that sound like a strange demand? If so, Paige took it in stride.

She tapped her pink nails on the counter. "Hold on. Let me check." She hurried into the backroom. I struggled not to nibble on my donut while she was gone. My willpower was weak when it came to my sweet tooth.

After a minute, she returned to the counter with a bag of peppermint candies. "Found these left over from Christmas. Will they do?" She peered into the bag. "They're old, so I won't charge you for them."

"Thanks, I appreciate it." I took the bags of peppermints and donuts back to my office, where Neville was apparently putting the finishing touches on my request.

"I thought you needed a donut to work," I said, and tossed the bag onto the table.

"I got inspired and ran with it," Neville replied. His gaze locked on the Boston cream donut. "Hello, gorgeous."

"That's a pretty necklace," I said.

He lifted the piece of gold jewelry from the table. It was a simple design with a dangling locket.

"What's in the locket?" I asked.

"The spell," he said. "While you're wearing the necklace, you close it to remain invisible and open it to be visible again."

"You're a genius." I took the necklace and slipped it over my head.

"Works like a charm," he joked.

"Are you sure?" I asked. "How can I tell?" I could still see myself.

Neville reached for a small mirror on a nearby shelf and

held it in front of me. Nothing. I was like a vampire. I opened the locket.

"There I am!" Egads. I sounded like my father playing peekaboo with Ryan.

"Every time you open and close the locket, you'll experience leakage," Neville warned.

I pulled a face. "Is there a less disgusting way of saying that?"

He laughed. "Sorry. It means that the spell will grow weaker the more you switch back and forth, so use it wisely. You don't want to end up visible at the wrong moment."

Well, duh.

"Thanks, Neville. This is awesome."

"And here is the other request," he said and handed me a silver chain. No locket on this one. "All you need to do is slip it over the supernatural's head and the spell activates."

"You're amazing, Neville. Thank you."

He blushed. "Anything else I can do to help before we go?"

"We?" I echoed. "No, there's no we. I go in search of the demon. You stay here and craft imaginative magical gizmos."

Neville began to pout. "Paul always promised me that one day he'd let me accompany him in the field."

"But that's not your lane, Neville. You need to stay in yours. It's safer."

He bowed his head. "Too right, my furious avenger."

I pointed a finger. "Please don't ever call me an avenger." It hit far too close to home.

"Yes, Agent Fury."

"The demon's already killed three. I don't need him to add you to the list. I only just started this job. I'd like to keep it for a bit longer."

"What about Chief Fox?" Neville asked. "Will you alert him to the perpetrator?"

"How can I? He won't understand an incorporeal demon."

I fingered the locket. "What did Pidcock do in these situations? I mean, Chief O'Neill was oblivious, so he clearly didn't confide in him."

"He worked solo in the field," Neville replied. "I wonder whether that made him an easier target for the fear demon."

"I doubt it," I said. "Chief O'Neill didn't tend to work solo and he didn't stand a chance."

"You have one thing in your favor," Neville said. "The element of surprise. None of his victims had that."

"True, and you can't fight what you can't see." My fingers curled around the locket. I hoped that was true, at least.

Because my life depended on it.

CHAPTER SEVENTEEN

THE LOCKET HUNG open around my neck as I worked in a hurry to set up the summoning circle. The wind was whipping my hair into a frenzy and I was relieved I'd be invisible soon. Not even a murdering demon needed to be subjected to this hairdo.

The vortex was in the heart of the triangle of land formed between the bay and the river. I parked on Manchego Place, the nearest road, and walked up to the strip of land with a backpack full of necessities.

First, I placed the rune rocks around the circle's perimeter. Once the runes were in the right order, I set down seven chunky white candles and lit them. I hadn't created a summoning circle by myself in years. When Anton and I were younger, we'd make them in the backyard and I'd place my Barbies in the middle as the offering. Cowboy Ken was usually the demon. I liked that he was a little bit sexy and dangerous. Normal Ken was too bland to be the demon. I would stick a knitted hat on him and pretend he was a gnome.

Today, instead of Barbies, I used peppermint candies. I

wasn't sure what the draw was for the fear demon—maybe he liked his breath minty fresh—but the book was a trusted resource so I went with it.

Once the circle was properly arranged, I sat cross-legged in the middle and began the incantation. If anyone caught a glimpse of me before I closed the locket, they'd think I was into weird yoga and keep their distance.

"Guardians of the underworld, hear my cries. Guardians of the overworld, hear my cries. Guardians of the otherworld, hear my cries."

The wind picked up steam again and I had to spit out the strands of hair that kept finding their way into my mouth. Note to self: next time I summon a demon, bring a scrunchie.

Another gust of wind rushed past and blew out the candles I'd carefully lit. Great. No one talks about the hazards of nature when trying to perform an outdoor ritual. I had to relight the candles or the summoning wouldn't work. If I failed to trap him, the demon would create his own circle and reform, free to walk out again. I couldn't let that happen. Enough people were already dead thanks to him.

I just managed to fix the candles when I felt a dramatic drop in temperature.

He was here.

Further along the shoreline, a figure materialized out of thin air, shrouded in dark energy. He wasn't corporeal yet, more like a ghost with an extra layer of padding. He moved toward the circle as though he knew it was there. As he drew closer, I saw his eyes and flinched. Red flames burned within the sockets. I clamped down on my fear before he sensed it. I didn't want to make him stronger than he already was.

The demon halted. His gaze swept across the grassy area until it alighted on the circle.

He smiled and I bit the inside of my cheek to keep from screaming.

His teeth were pointy and undoubtedly razor sharp. Were they deadly in their altered state? I didn't want to find out. Why a demon that fed on fear needed sharp teeth, I had no idea. It seemed biologically unnecessary.

Stay grounded, Eden. I wanted to smack myself. *No one cares about your biological ruminations when there's a fear demon on the loose.*

The demon began to take exaggerated steps toward the circle. "Come out, come out, wherever you are," he called. Despite his frightful appearance, he sounded more like the host of a children's show than a dangerous fear demon.

I remained quiet in the middle of the circle, though my heart hammered so loudly in my chest, I was sure that the entire town could hear it. The peppermints were free of the bag, now scattered around the rune rocks. I just needed him to enter the circle so I could keep him here.

"I sense your fears." He stopped again and inhaled deeply, which seemed like a waste of effort since he still lacked lungs. "They are so very powerful."

If he thinks this fear is powerful, he should catch up with me during a mammogram.

"Your family," he said. "Your very nature scares you. It's truly delicious. I can draw it out of you. Make it real. It tastes best when the fear is real."

That's right, Mr. Fear Demon. Come closer.

His silhouette seemed to grow more solid with each step.

"I wish I had encountered you sooner," he said. "With energy like yours, I would have regained my true form by now."

Ugh. He was feeding off me. I tried to focus on other thoughts. On the innocent lives he took—Chief O'Neill. Paul Pidcock. Elliott. My fear turned to anger and outrage.

He spotted a peppermint and crossed the threshold. "What is this delectable treat?" When he bent over to retrieve the candy, I stepped gingerly outside the circle and popped open the locket.

"Do us all a favor and eat one," I said. "We'd rather die of our fears than your rancid breath."

His mouth split into a ferocious smile. "Ah, the witty banter portion of the evening." He stopped talking and cocked his head. "What happened to your hair?"

Instinctively, my hand flew to smooth my unruly locks. "The wind I stirred up, okay? My hair is thin, but I have a lot of it, so it gets crazy."

"You might want to consider a ponytail next time."

"Thanks for the tip, Vidal Sassoon."

"Perhaps I can improve it for you." He took a step toward me, but an invisible force pushed him back inside the circle.

"No can do, Vidal."

The demon glanced around wildly, realizing his mistake in entering the circle. "No!" The red flames of his eyes grew brighter. He pinned his fiery gaze on me. "I may not be able to touch you, but I can still reach you."

Black wings sprouted from my back. Sweet Hecate! He was using his demon mojo on me to bring my fears to life. My head began to pound with cries of insanity. I wasn't expecting that. I closed my eyes and tried to fight the pulsating sounds.

"Let me go or I'll suck you dry," the demon said.

I forced open my eyes and saw that his body was hardening. The ritual was working.

"You knew what would happen to those men when you forced them toward their fears. You could have just taken the energy and let them live, but you didn't."

"Of course I didn't," he said. "I *wanted* them to die. Those last moments before death are the most powerful. Each one brought me closer to my former self."

"Too bad your former self is right back in a tiny prison."

He glared at me. "I will extract so much energy from you that they'll have to scrape your remains off the ground."

"I think you'll find it's the other way around." The air whirled around the demon as the remainder of the spell took hold, locking him in place. I listened to his long string of profanities and hoped no one came to investigate the uproar. The rest of my task was easy. One thrust of the hemlock stick in my pocket and the demon would cease to exist. He was a killer. He deserved it. His death was for the best—a favor to humanity.

And yet.

Neville's disapproving tone echoed in my head. He was right. It wasn't my job to carry out punishment. That was my dark side rearing its head—trying to coax me into a role as judge, jury, *and* executioner.

But I don't want to be the villain of my own story. I want to be the hero. I've always wanted to be the hero. When we played games as children, my brother and cousins always chose the most evil creatures imaginable and I always chose the white knight or the Disney princess or Buffy. (I was alone in my love for the vampire slayer television show. My family only tolerated the episodes when Angel turned full vampire. They felt like they finally had a character to root for.) I want to save, not destroy.

The demon's rampage was over. He was trapped and vulnerable because I'd won. If I killed him now, what did that make me?

The air calmed and the fear demon stood before me in a completely solid state, naked, the fire in his eyes reduced to embers.

I could've done without the naked part.

He dropped to his knees, and I breathed a sigh of relief. The top of his head was a better view.

"Do your worst, fury," he said. His chin jerked up in defiance. Whatever I had planned for him, he was ready. He'd seen and experienced people's worst fears. Absorbed the energy and fed off it. There was nothing I could do that would impact him in any meaningful way.

I took a step closer and met his gaze. "I'm not going to kill you," I said, and my wings promptly dissipated.

"Why not? I would've killed you." He peered at me. "Why aren't you going to kill me?"

"Because that's not who I am."

He snorted. "I beg to differ, fury. I felt your spirit. Your restless energy. It's exactly who you are. You cannot fight the will of the gods, girl. If it is their will that you be a fury, then so be it."

I tossed the hemlock stick aside. "But I don't have to *act* like one," I said. "It's our choices that define us, not our genetics or the will of any god."

He splayed his hands. "Well, that's disappointing."

I ignored him and took out my phone to call FBM headquarters. Once the call was made, I tucked the phone in my pocket.

"Now there's one more thing I need to do." I pulled from my pocket the second chain that Neville made around his neck to make the demon appear human to anyone without the Sight.

"Good work, Eden." My father's voice startled me.

I swiveled to face him. "Dad? What are you doing here?"

He gestured to the cowering fear demon with the hemlock stick he must've retrieved from the ground. "Just wanted to see you in action. I've never had the chance to watch you work. It's impressive."

"Thanks." I watched him warily. "I'm going to make him look human now. Then the FBM can collect him from Chief Fox. We'll say he's being taken to a maximum security prison." This way the town would get closure. The humans didn't need to know the demon would end up back in Other-world where he belonged.

My father grunted. I knew that sound. Dissatisfaction. I'd recognize it in my sleep because I'd heard it from him my entire life.

"What's wrong with my plan?" I asked.

"What happens when he leaves the circle?" my father asked. "The binding is only good when he's in there."

"Your father's right," the demon said. "You can make me look human, but I'll still be me."

I glared at the demon. "Whose side are you on?"

He shrugged. "Whichever side frees me, I guess."

My father rolled up his sleeves. "I'll do the honors."

"Dad!"

He motioned to the fear demon with the stick. "Go on. Finish whatever you're doing. Far be it for me to interrupt an agent's important work."

I hesitated before turning back to the fear demon and placing the chain around his neck. Poof! A nondescript middle-aged man stood before us. Fully clothed. Phew.

My father moved to stand beside me and I noticed that his skin was glowing red. The vengeance demon was gearing up for action.

"What do you think you're doing?" I said.

"Mick was my good friend," my father said. "I'm a vengeance demon. What did you think would happen?" He raised his hand and I knew what he intended to do with the hemlock stick.

"No. This isn't right." I tugged his arm.

"Isn't it?" My father looked at me askance. "Ask Mick's friends and family. Ask Elliott's wife. Ask Paul Pidcock's—well, I don't think that guy had anybody, but you get the idea."

"I can't let you kill him. How would we explain it to the

new chief?" How would I explain it to headquarters when I'd already called them?

"You think I care about explaining our ways to Chief Fox?"

"Of course you care," I said. "You were friends with Chief O'Neill for years. That relationship wouldn't have been possible if you didn't care." I stepped between my father and the circle, blocking his access to the demon. "If you want to kill him, you have to kill me first."

My father's eyes bore into mine. "There's no reason to let him live, Eden."

"Maybe that's an argument some people could make about you," I replied. "But I wouldn't let anyone kill you either."

"Agent Fury?"

Double-decker crap sandwich.

Chief Fox was hurrying across the grass to reach us. My father's red glow faded. I glanced at the fear demon and noticed his smirk. My father was right. The moment the demon left the circle, he'd try to feed off the chief's fears. Or mine. I had to act.

I reached into the circle and gripped the demon's shoulder. It hurt like hell, but I drew in his power. Anything to weaken the demon so that he could be transported out of the circle without hurting anyone. Once the FBM team arrived, they'd have special cuffs to keep him from throwing his power around. Come to think of it, I should probably request a set. They would've come in handy here.

Chief Fox arrived at the scene and frowned at the circle. "What's going on?"

"This is your killer, Chief," my father said. "He confessed. We stopped him before he could target his next victim."

Chief Fox examined the strange setup of the rune rocks and peppermints. "Is he a Satan worshipper or something?"

"Yes, I think so," my father said.

I released the demon and staggered forward from the rush of energy. "I've called the feds," I managed to say. Of course I didn't specify which feds, so it wasn't technically a lie. "They'll meet you here to take him off your hands." It took all my strength to respond and sound normal. The fear demon's power was surging inside me, wreaking havoc on my system. My chest tightened and I wanted to scream. The negative energy was agonizing.

"Maybe we should call a paramedic," Chief Fox said. "Do we know what happened to him? He looks half dead."

My father seemed to sense my inner turmoil. "Whatever it was, he did it to himself," he said. "We found him like this."

Chief Fox stooped down and lifted a peppermint from the ground. He sniffed the wrapper. "Weird. I don't associate peppermints with satanic rituals."

"Even the devil appreciates fresh breath," I said through gritted teeth. I felt ready to vomit from the overload of fear coursing through my veins.

The chief gave me a concerned look. "You look unwell, Agent Fury. Why don't you go and I'll take it from here? We can talk about what happened later."

"I'll take her home," my father offered. "My car's real close." He hooked an arm around my waist and escorted me away from the circle.

"Thanks," I wheezed. My head was spinning.

"You siphoned too much," he said quietly.

"No choice," I croaked. I barely made it to the car before I passed out.

CHAPTER EIGHTEEN

IT TOOK me a full twenty-four hours to recover from the demon's energy. I was just glad that I managed to hold on for as long as I did. I knew from headquarters that the fear demon had been taken into FBM custody and returned to Otherworld. I still worried that Chief Fox would ask questions I couldn't answer. His presence in town promised to make my job more complicated than I'd like.

My mother appeared to take great pleasure in my weakened state and sent Verity to the attic several times to check on me and came once on her own with a tube of lipstick to see if I wanted to look 'presentable.' Anton also brought Ryan up to share his cookie with me, which ended up getting crushed under my cheek on the pillow. Even my grandmother's cat displayed a modicum of concern. Candy left a dead mouse at the bottom of the mattress, which I discovered when I stretched out my bare foot in the middle of the night. Other than horrible nightmares, though, I was relatively unscathed.

The moment I decided to leave the solitude of the attic, I knew it was a mistake.

"Charlemagne, let go of the bear." Although Verity's voice was calm, I detected an undercurrent of fear.

I poked my head into the family room. Verity had Charlemagne cornered. The python had its jaws wrapped around a brown teddy bear. Ryan was bawling in his bouncer in the middle of the family room floor, while Grandma dozed on one end of the couch and Olivia read a book on the other. My mother was engrossed in the television, oblivious to the chaos around her.

"I'm alive," I said, waving my hands in front of me.

"That's terrific, honey." My mother kept her gaze pinned on the television screen. "Clara stopped by to see you earlier, but I told her you were sleeping."

"Hi, Eden," Verity said. "I'm so glad you're up and about. I hate to ask, but would you mind helping me rescue Mr. Cuddles?"

Charlemagne shook the bear back and forth and Olivia giggled from the couch. "Mr. Cuddles is going to throw up if Charlemagne keeps shaking him like that."

"Mr. Cuddles isn't real," Verity said. "He can't throw up."

Olivia concentrated on the soft toy. "Maybe there's a way to make him."

Verity drew a steadying breath. "Drop it, Charlemagne."

"Just take it from him and stop interrupting my nap," Grandma said, suddenly awake. "He's a snake. What harm can he do?"

"If it's so easy, then you do it," Verity snapped.

Everyone in the room froze. No one took that tone with my grandmother. Verity seemed to realize her error. She straightened her blouse and looked my grandmother in the eye.

"Apologies, Grandma," the druid said. "It's just hard to think straight with my son crying. It stresses me out."

Ryan had paused momentarily, but apparently only to

gain strength. His renewed wailing cries brought Aunt Thora in from the garden.

"What on earth is happening in here?" My great-aunt stood in the doorframe, holding a basket of lemons. She walked straight over to Ryan and popped one into his open mouth. The crying immediately ceased.

"Aunt Thora, that's a lemon," Verity said, aghast.

"A very versatile fruit," Aunt Thora said.

Verity watched with interest as Ryan took the lemon out of his mouth and examined it with large, round eyes. He licked the side, testing it. The bear was now forgotten.

"He must take after my side of the family," Aunt Thora said, beaming.

"It's entirely possible since he still doesn't show any aptitude for…anything," Grandma said.

"He's a year old," I said. "Give him time."

"Eden's right," my mom said. "She's twenty-six and we're still giving her time."

"Charlemagne, no!" Olivia said, as the snake's fangs plunged into the bear's soft body.

My mother abandoned her show. "Oh, for Nyx's sake." She extended a hand toward the snake. "Mother of darkness, take great care. Exert your will and bring me the bear."

The bear shook loose from the snake's mouth and shot into my mother's outstretched hand. I shook my head before shuffling into the kitchen and getting a glass of water to take back up to the attic. Two minutes downstairs and my head was already beginning to hurt.

I climbed up the attic steps, careful not to spill my water. I could still hear chaos below. Apparently, the bear had lost some of its stuffing. Aunt Thora promised to fix it.

I placed the glass on the floor and crawled onto the mattress.

"Peace and quiet again." I relaxed against the mattress.

"What was that, Eden?" Alice's transparent head popped out of a box. "You aren't experiencing more nightmares, are you? It was dreadful listening to you. Your screams are very convincing."

I groaned and pulled the covers over my head.

"I see you'd like privacy," Alice said. "I was hoping you could regale me with stories of the fear demon. How did you manage to catch him?"

"I'd love to tell you all about it, Alice, but maybe later. If you don't mind, I'd like some time alone to gather my thoughts."

"I completely understand," Alice said. "There's no place like home sweet home to reconnect with yourself, is there?" She made a big show of swishing around the attic before disappearing into the darkness.

"Yes, home sweet home," I murmured, plumping my pillow.

And then there was the sweet sound of silence.

I waited until later that afternoon to return to work, to make sure I was fully operational.

"Rejoice! The kindly one returns." Neville welcomed me back in the office with a chocolate glazed donut and a cup of coffee. I inhaled the rich aroma.

"This isn't from Holes," I said.

"No, I went to the Daily Grind first," Neville said. "But Paige carefully selected the donut for you."

"Thank you both," I said, and bit into the donut. It tasted delicious.

"I received your text yesterday and I also took the liberty of ordering two sets of special cuffs from headquarters," Neville said. "They should arrive within the week."

"That long?"

"It's FBM headquarters, not Amazon Prime," he replied.

"You're a dream, Neville. Thanks." I paused. "Why didn't Paul have any cuffs? I would think it's a necessity."

"He used to, but he lost them in the bay two years ago when he was wrangling a kelpie gone mad. Neither of us thought to replace them. We haven't needed them often."

"Well, they'll make a good addition to our office," I said.

"I've been wanting to ask you," Neville began carefully. "Have you picked up any new talents as a result of your interactions with the fear demon?"

"You mean did I gain a new fury power?"

He nodded.

"No, not this time."

"Why not?" Neville asked. "Forgive the intrusive question, but I find your case fascinating."

I bristled. "I'm not a case, Neville." I sat behind my desk and sipped my coffee. It was heavenly. "My siphoning power comes from my mother's side, so I don't automatically get a fury power just from using it. I think it happened in San Francisco because I became a vampire and bit Fergus. A malevolent act. It just so happened that the siphoning power was the reason I did it."

"If you say so," he replied. He didn't sound convinced.

"Look, there's no fury handbook, so it's not like all this stuff is written down for me. It's based on what I've read and my experiences so far."

"Well, I, for one, look forward to joining you on this exploratory journey, O furious one."

"Thanks, Neville. It's nice to have someone on my team." Someone who wasn't trying to guilt me or mock me for wanting to be *good*.

A knock on the door startled both of us. I glanced around wildly in case there was something to hide.

ANNABEL CHASE

"No worries," Neville whispered. "The office is cloaked to look normal to humans without the Sight."

That was a relief because Neville had jars of potions scattered across the table in the back. I had no clue what he was working on, but it looked like quite the project.

Neville opened the door and Chief Fox walked in, followed by Sean. The deputy held a long pole in one hand and a coffee cup in the other.

Chief Fox flashed a megawatt smile that instantly got my blood pumping. "I hope you're feeling better, Agent Fury."

"I am, thanks," I said. A little weak in the knees, but that was a given when Chief Fox was in the room.

He scanned the barebones room and frowned. "I thought you were in the cyber crime division?" He scratched the back of his head. "Shouldn't there be more high tech gear in here?"

I moved to block his view of the outdated computer on my desk. "We have to make it look like a typical office," I said quickly. "Otherwise, we'd be a target for tech thieves."

Chief Fox peered at me. "That's a thing, huh?"

"Oh, yes, sir," Neville piped up. "The same groups that break into Apple stores and steal as many devices as they can, they'll also target field offices with expensive computer systems."

Sean snorted. "Maybe you should think about putting a lock on the front door then."

I glared at the deputy. "Did I mention we investigate online fraud and child porn?"

Sean glowered at me.

"I brought you a present," the chief said. "A token of appreciation for helping catch the killer." He elbowed the deputy, who seemed to forget he came bearing the gift.

"It's a sun lamp." Sean put his coffee cup on my desk and placed the lamp on the floor next to it.

"You mentioned how dark your office is..." Chief Fox

trailed off as he surveyed the dismal space. "And now I see what you mean."

A thrill shot through me. He remembered that? "Thank you so much, Chief." This was one of the most thoughtful presents anyone had ever given me.

"If you're feeling up to it, maybe we can talk about what happened by the bay," the chief said.

"There isn't much to tell," I lied. "My dad and I were taking a walk and we found him in that weird circle. He was raving like a lunatic, talking about killing more people for his master, the devil. Then he sort of collapsed."

"So he *was* a Satan worshipper." Sean smacked the chief on the arm. "Good call, Chief."

The chief stared at the spot on his arm where the deputy had smacked him. I had a feeling Sean wouldn't be doing that again.

"I heard you fainted," Sean said. I didn't miss the taunting note in his voice. "No wonder you got sent packing from your old job." He picked up his coffee cup from my desk.

Chief Fox gave him a hard look. "I read in your file that it took you three tries to get your driver's license."

I smothered a laugh. "I remember that!"

Sean's cheeks flamed. "It was raining the first time. It was distracting!"

"What about the second time?" I asked.

He glared at me. "I don't know why you think you're so special, Eden. If you were, Tanner wouldn't have cheated on you with Sassy."

My jaw clenched.

"Who's Tanner?" Chief Fox asked.

"A guy we went to high school with," I explained.

"Is he still local?" Chief Fox asked.

"Sure is," Sean said. "He's a great guy. I'll introduce you."

"Please do," the chief said, in a tone that suggested Tanner might walk away from that introduction with a parking ticket.

"Have you met Sassy, Chief?" Sean continued. "You definitely want to, if you catch my meaning."

Quickly, I wrote out a spell on the side of my leg. To anyone else, it looked like I was scratching an itch, but I knew better.

Sean sipped his coffee and grimaced. "What the hell? How did butter get in my coffee?" He slapped the lid back on the cup. "I'm going to complain."

"I think we've taken up enough of your time," Chief Fox said. "If you think of anything else, will you let me know?"

"Sure. Thanks again for the lamp."

Once they left, I plugged in the lamp and turned it on.

"How'd the butter get in his coffee?" Neville asked. "Was that you?"

I smiled. "A simple spell my grandmother taught me as a kid. I used it on the high school principal more times than I care to admit." I avoided spells like that now, mostly because they tended to indulge my dark side—or my immature side. I wasn't proud of either one.

"Chief Fox seems to like you," Neville remarked. He moved to the table to continue whatever experiments he was doing.

"I think he wants to see me as an asset." Which wasn't a bad thing. Not at all.

"I think he wants to see your ass," Neville said. He quickly clamped his hand over his mouth. "Did I say that out loud? Sorry, O benevolent one."

I swiveled my chair to face him. "Neville, I know you find my situation fascinating, but I'm trying to forget I'm a fury. I didn't want this job and I'm trying to make the best of it, which also means staying as close to normal as humanly possible." I sighed. "It would help if you...helped."

Neville bowed his head. "For what it's worth, I think you make a wonderful fury. From what I've seen so far, this world is lucky to have you on its side."

I tapped the necklace still around my throat. "You, too. Your charm worked...like a charm." I unclasped the necklace and placed it on my desk. "Probably best not to wear it on a regular basis, though."

Neville grinned. "There's plenty more where that came from, O angry one." He cleared his throat. "I mean, Agent Fury."

"Eden," I said. "Just Eden will do."

* * *

Don't miss the next book in the series — **Fury Godmother**, *Federal Bureau of Magic Cozy Mystery, Book 2.*

Thank you for reading *Great Balls of Fury*! If you sign up for my newsletter, you can receive FREE short stories. https://www.annabelchase.com

Other series by Annabel Chase include:

Starry Hollow Witches

Spellbound Paranormal Cozy Mysteries

Midnight Empire

Pandora's Pride

Spellslingers Academy

Magic Bullet

Demonspawn Academy